THE WICKED PRINCE

NEW YORK TIMES BESTSELLING AUTHOR
CLAIRE CONTRERAS

The Wicked Prince
Claire Contreras
© 2021 Claire Contreras
Cover design By Hang Le
Edited by Erica Russikoff
Proofread by Janice Owen
Formatted by Champagne Book Design

THE WICKED PRINCE

CHAPTER ONE

JOSLYN

I NEVER HATED PARTIES UNTIL I BECAME A HANDLER OF SORTS for Prince Aramis. Now, hearing the word *party* makes my anxiety soar. I despise him. And parties. But mostly him for making me hate parties. I shouldered past a woman, then another, and another. They're all wearing sequins and their dresses are so short I'd bet money he'd already seen all of their privates, though that was easy money. After all, this was Aramis we were talking about. Playboy of the century. Partier for the ages. He was quintessentially Jay Gatsby in modern day, if Jay Gatsby had been a prince and had everything and everyone at their beck and call. When I first met Aramis, I'd fallen head over heels for him. At first sight. These days, thinking back on that time, I knew it was because I'd gone to an all-girl school all my life and had very little exposure to boys. When you live in a bubble and with little experiences with boys and meet one in the midst of your hormones raging, well, let's just say losing my virginity to the one and only Aramis had been a no-brainer. Thankfully, of all the crude annoyances that came out of his mouth, that experience wasn't one of them. I had to give at least that much to the man—he had a little bit of respect for me.

"Oh, there she is, the bitch in red," he shouted upon my entrance.

A little bit of respect for me. A little bit. I sighed heavily, turning the lights on, walking over to the table and switching the multicolor stage lights off and unplug-ging the DJ's speakers—back, to back, to back, to back. Everyone groaned and complained all at once. I looked around at all of them—disgusting, sweating, inebriated, drugged out, dancing, fucking, sinful creatures, and shook my head, as if I were their mother. Rather than be mad at myself for being this prudish, I turned my glare on Aramis, who was sitting in a chair, much like a throne, with one leg propped up and the other on the floor, a goofy drunken smile on his face.

"Everyone, get out," I said loudly, still staring at him.

"Aw, but the party was just getting started, Boss," he said.

"Out," I shouted. "Out, out, out, out, out!"

"On whose orders?" a random guy shouted from somewhere in the room.

"By order of The Crown. Do you need me to have you arrested?" I yelled even louder.

Everyone seemed to get a clue and rushed out of the room.

"I need to put my things away." That was the DJ.

"It's fine." I kicked away an empty beer can and walked over to Aramis, standing a few feet away from him. "You're supposed to stay home healing."

"I'm home." He sat up in the chair with a flinch. "Fuck, that hurt."

I shut my eyes briefly before turning around and fetching him a water bottle from the small refrigerator in the corner of the room. I hated that he dealt with pain by getting drunk and high and God only knew what else. The only thing Aramis wasn't using to ease his pain these days were women and I had a feeling it was because he didn't love what he saw in the mirror. The fiery car accident he'd been in a couple of months ago had changed him in that sense at least. If I was being honest with myself, I felt bad for him and a part of me wished he would go back to being the playboy who slept around. Mostly, I just wanted him to calm down so that I wouldn't have all of this responsibility weighing on my shoulders. I grabbed a glass water bottle and twisted the cap off as I walked over to him.

"I had to leave my date with David early because of

this party." I handed him the bottle. He closed his hand over mine and pulled me closer with the bottle. I gasped in surprise, my heart hammering. I hated when he did things like that.

"Your date with David?" he asked, his alcohol-infused breath tickling my nose. I pulled back and tried handing him the bottle again. This time, he took it without pulling me along.

"Yes, my date with David."

"Why were you on a date with David?"

"Why do you care?"

"I don't." He frowned and made a face like he had a bad taste in his mouth. "Still. David."

I didn't know what was worse, the fact that he acted like a jealous boyfriend or the fact that he acted that way but never showed any interest in me otherwise. I had to assume this jealousy thing was just him being bitter about the fact that maybe I had someone and he had nobody at all. Yet another reason why finding him a match was a good idea.

"Well, you need to be ready tomorrow. We're all going to Versailles for the next few weeks and I personally would rather not make the commute back and forth for dumb things, so please make sure you pack everything you need." I stepped away and started walking back toward the door.

"Help me pack."

"Why?" I groaned, throwing my head back. I should have known this was coming.

"I'm no good at packing; you don't want to make the commute. Help me pack."

"Fine." I walked past him and headed straight toward his bedroom.

Aramis didn't live in a palace, but he might as well have. He had two entire apartment floors to himself. Everyone in the royal family lived this way. It was a downgrade from a palace, but a definite upgrade from the way everyone else lived. My three-hundred-square-foot flat was the size of just one of Aramis's closets, and he had a lot of them. I walked over to his luggage closet, that was big enough to hold ten people's travel equipment and their emotional baggage all in one. Rolling two suitcases out of there, I walked back to his bedroom and lay them out on the floor.

"You don't expect me to pack your underwear for you as well, do you?" I called out. "Because that's where I draw the line."

"It wouldn't be the first time you've seen my underwear." He walked into the room, finishing off the water in his hand.

"Are you going to keep reminding me of the mistake I made when I was a teenager?"

"Mistake?" His eyebrows shot up. "Once is a mistake. Three times . . . well, I think most would consider that a habit."

"Habits can be mistakes too." I smiled at him. "I mean, look at all the people who smoke cigarettes."

"Now you're comparing me to things that can kill you?" He smirked. "Should I be flattered?"

I sighed, refusing to answer him. Truth be told, if I didn't know him as well as I did, I might just consider Aramis a deadly weapon. It was the way he looked at you, the way he smiled, the way he held everyone's attention with little effort. He was smart, funny, charming, and wicked sexy. All things I had to ignore every single day while I was around him because despite all of those things, he was also a heartbreaker. He ran through women the way Olympians ran across finish lines. That was his sport. And I couldn't handle being another notch on his bedpost.

CHAPTER TWO

ARAMIS

MY HEAD WAS KILLING ME AND THE FACT THAT MY MOTHER couldn't get a clue and stop talking wasn't helping. I'd tuned her out halfway through her rant about my behavior, which was difficult to do since we were sharing a car to Versailles. She talked about me as if I was an impertinent child who needed to be put in timeout. I tried not to let it get to me. The only reason I'd agreed to even come to Versailles for holiday was because I could leave any time I wanted. Elias always had a helicopter on the pad, waiting to cater to his guests, and if I felt the need to take a little trip out of there I would. It wasn't like any of us liked being there. It was haunted. I wasn't going to say no though. Not when my sister-in-law, Addie, was due to give birth any minute. The little prince would be my first nephew and I couldn't wait to meet him.

"Mother, please drop it." I sighed, closing my eyes and massaging my head.

"I asked Joslyn to make a list of potential girlfriends for you."

"What?" My eyes popped open. "Why?"

"Because enough is enough, Aramis. You've lived the playboy life and now it's time for you to at least pretend to settle down."

"So this is all for pretenses then?" I shook my head. "This is exactly why the people don't like us, because they think we're fakers."

"We're not fakers. Your brother is genuinely in love with Adeline."

"Right. Tell me again, Mother, how thrilled you were about him finding love with a commoner."

"Aramis." She glared at me. "I love Adeline like a daughter."

"Because she's your Queen and not loving her like a daughter would mean you'd be thrown to the wolves." I couldn't help my smile. My mother really did love Addie like a daughter, but I loved to rile her up.

"Aramis. That's enough. You will let Joslyn vet these women and you will go on dates with the ones she chooses."

"On whose orders? Yours?"

"By order of The Crown."

"My brother is okay with this?" I scoffed. "Yeah right. Eli was just as much a playboy as I am."

"Your brother cannot afford any more headlines with you kicking out heiresses in the middle of the night. You need to settle down or become a monk. Either one would benefit us right now."

"Fine. A life of solitude it is." I closed my eyes and rested my head against the window.

"Joslyn will have a list to you by tomorrow."

"Will she be on that list?" I was almost drifting off as I asked the question.

"Joslyn?" My mother laughed. "She wouldn't date you if you were the last man on Earth."

"Why do you say that?" My eyes popped open.

"Because you're a nightmare around her." She shrugged. "Besides, she has a boyfriend. He's joining us here for the weekend."

"David is coming?"

"Yes. Why the face? I thought you liked David. He's wonderful."

"I do like David." I felt myself scowl. "I just don't like David for Joss."

My mother looked at me for a long, silent moment, her amused expression quickly turning into horror. "Oh, no, Aramis. Absolutely not. You can date whomever you want but you stay the bloody hell away from Joslyn. She's a nice girl and she's doing splendid work as your sister's secretary. I refuse to lose her to your childish antics."

"You're right. It would be such a shame if I made her fall for me."

"She's with David." There was a shrill to my mother's voice, as if she knew what I was thinking.

Truth was, I didn't know what I was thinking and I didn't know why I hated the thought of Joslyn being with David. It was stupid. Despite my being a jerk to her most of the time, I cared about Joslyn. I wanted her to be happy. She deserved to be happy. Maybe my mother was right. Maybe it was time for me to find someone to settle down with. Joslyn couldn't be the one for me. I knew that all those years ago when we hooked up and I knew that now. Unfortunately, it didn't make me want her any less.

CHAPTER THREE

JOSLYN

H E HAD A THING FOR THE UNATTAINABLE. IT WAS THE MAIN reason I was focusing on those for the short list I was putting together of potential women he could date. I wasn't sure if you can call a list of twelve women short, but it was what it was. Aramis was impossible to keep content. If anyone knew that it was me. I was his sister, Pilar's, secretary, but had been helping him for the last few months while she lay low with her fiancé Ben. I was juggling her wedding and Aramis's attitude as he recovered from the car accident he suffered, and I wasn't sure which was more stressful. Not to say that Pilar was a bridezilla, and being so involved in planning my best friend's wedding was fun, but dealing with vendors and babysitting a grown man were getting to me. It was one of the reasons I was so relieved when Adeline called me to tell me we'd be spending the Christmas holiday in Versailles. It was secluded and there was no possible way Aramis could get in any kind of trouble out here. There were no heiresses nearby, no press, no paparazzi, no one he could legitimately upset, which in turn meant no mess for me to clean up. I could finally just focus on my two best friends and what they had going for them right now. One of them was getting married and the other was having a baby in two months and I was overjoyed by both. Of course, my joy didn't mean I didn't stop and question what I had going for myself and why I wasn't on the same timeline, but that was okay too. I'd come to terms with the fact that I could be genuinely happy for them and still want more for myself.

I'd been seeing David for a month now and even though it was an extremely short amount of time and we were still getting to know each other, I knew he wasn't the man I would marry. It just didn't seem like settling down was high on his list of priorities. Every time we talked about our friends settling down, he made a joke and said he hoped that wouldn't be him. I liked David though. I liked spending time with him. He was funny, smart, charismatic, and handsome. As the car came to a stop, I looked out the window and saw Aramis holding the door open for his mother. My heart did a little jiggle. I hated that. I hated the fact that seeing him always elicited some kind of unwanted emotion out of me. Forget the fact that I'd been seeing him for ten years now. Forget the fact that he was a total asshole to me. Forget the fact that I had to endure seeing him with women every other day and pretend I didn't care. Well, I didn't. I didn't actually care. I just . . . I paused, frowning at my own thoughts. Did I care? I didn't. There was a lot to be said about the person you gave your virginity to, that was all. I'd never forget the experiences we had together and that was okay. I'd also never forget that after the third time we slept together I caught him making out with one of my college roommates. That was the emotion I liked to cling onto most when I was around him. It wasn't hate, not anymore, but I was cautious.

The driver stopped directly behind Aramis's car and got down as I gathered my things. When he opened the door, Aramis looked at me and my heart did that little skip again. Dammit. Thankfully, David was meeting me here for a few days. That would take my mind off this weird situation I was facing. Falling for a member of the royal family would be stupid, falling for my boss would be disastrous, falling for the man who broke my heart all those years ago was unthinkable. As I walked over, I said hi to his mother with a kiss on each cheek.

"You look wonderful. When did you get sun? I haven't seen it in months."

"Sunless tan. It's the best invention I've come across recently." I smiled.

"I tried that once. I ended up looking like an orange."

She laughed as she started to walk. I glanced over at Aramis, who was just standing there, staring.

"Hey, Aramis."

"Joslyn." He gave a nod, looking at me from beneath those long, dark lashes of his as I passed him and followed behind his mother.

"I heard David is due for a visit," his mother said. "That will be nice. Pilar, Ben, and you two can double date while he's here. I wonder if you can get one of the bachelorettes on the list to join you with Aramis."

"I'm sure I can make something work."

"I'm standing right here you know?" Aramis's voice cut through our conversation.

"Oh, love, you know it's for your own good." His mother smiled. "Let Joslyn help you."

"Yeah, let me help." I smiled over at him.

"If you're so worried about my image, why don't you go on a date with me, Joslyn?"

"I . . . what?" My heart stopped beating.

"Don't listen to him. He knows we highly discourage staff from dating the family.

"Why?" Aramis seemed genuinely confused.

"It's in the contract. To protect her and The Crown." His mother was looking at him like he'd lost his marbles. I tried not to laugh. "There used to be a clause in the contract about it until Elias came along and did away with it."

"There was a clause specifically forbidding our employees to date me?"

"Not just you. Anyone here."

"Who wrote that in the contracts?" he asked.

"Your father. Years ago. Like I said, Elias did away with it, though I wish he hadn't." She waved him off. "I'm going to look for your brother and Adeline before I go walk the gardens. See you later, Joslyn." She smiled and walked away as I waved and looked around.

Standing inside of Versailles was never going to be normal. It was too grand, too majestic, too much. It was one thing to visit during field trips at school, but being here as a guest was impossible to get used to. Adeline felt the same way and she was Queen now, so I wasn't sure I'd ever get used to standing here as a guest. The couple of times I'd stayed here had been in the guest cottages on the premises, which was where I'd be staying again. It seemed that as much as everyone loved the gardens, no one really wanted to sleep inside of the palace. Some said it was haunted and I had to agree, even though I hadn't personally seen anything.

"Did you know about the contract?" Aramis's voice cut through my thoughts. I turned to him with a frown.

"What?"

"The contract. Did you know there was a clause that forbids you from dating a member of the family or a co-worker?"

"Yes. I mean, I signed the contract, Aramis." I laughed, shaking my head. "It's really not a big deal."

"You don't think so?"

"No. Why would I?" I shrugged a shoulder and started walking in the direction of the back doors, hoping I saw either Pilar or Adeline on my way there.

"They shouldn't dictate what you do in your personal time."

"Why does it matter to you?" I met his gaze. "You never cared about any of it before."

"I didn't know this before."

"Why does it matter now?"

"It doesn't. Not to me. But you should care." His frown deepened.

"Well, I don't. I wasn't planning on dating anyone I work with."

"But now you can't even pretend to date me even if you wanted to."

"That's outrageous." I laughed loudly. "Why would I want to pretend to date you?"

"It would kill two birds with one stone. We pretend to date, the paparazzi finally backs off, and the royal family reputation is salvaged." He shrugged. "It's a lot easier than finding a woman on that list of yours I'd actually be interested in."

I stopped walking just before I reached the back doors, where I could see Pilar, Ben, Adeline, Elias, and his mother talking outside in the beginning of the gardens. Aramis stopped walking as well and turned to me as I faced him.

"Let me get this straight, you would rather pretend

date me than find out whether or not you're compatible with the women on the list I made you?"

"Yes."

"These are interesting women, Aramis. Beautiful women. Smart, and funny, and totally would fit the role of being your partner. Most of them are already in the limelight."

"I'm not interested."

I searched his eyes as he searched mine and I knew he was serious, I just didn't understand why. He loved women. Loved to date, loved to charm the panties off of women, literally, so why not date these?

"I'm going to send you the list and you can let me know which ones you approve of," I said.

"Why don't we go through the list together?"

"That's fine."

"Maybe you should set up interviews and sit with me in the room while I ask questions."

"Sure." I frowned.

"Really? You don't think any of this is bullshit?" He scoffed. "I'm supposed to find love in a list and perform interviews?"

"In all fairness, they didn't say you needed to find love."

"Right. Just a woman who could save my reputation and keep me out of trouble."

"I know it sounds awful. Trust me, I get why you want to avoid all of it, but The Crown can't afford any bad press right now and while Elias and Addie having a baby is taking a lot of the attention, it's a double-edged sword for you. Your younger sister is getting married, your older brother is having a baby, and guess who the attention is going to fall on when those things happen?"

"I hate this." He glanced away. "I never asked to be born a prince."

"You're right. You didn't. You loved reaping all of the benefits of it up until this point though. You need to step up. You'll be fine." I offered him a small smile. "I think this is the first civil conversation we've ever had."

"We have civil conversations all the time."

"Do we? I feel like we're always arguing."

"You call that arguing?" He smiled. "I call it foreplay."

My heart skipped. "I prefer my foreplay to be a little more physical."

"I can arrange that."

"No. You can't." I shot him a look as I stepped forward to open the door, reminding myself to keep breathing, that he didn't mean any of this. Aramis was only always trying to get a rise out of me. "I'll send you the list. We'll go over it tomorrow."

"Tonight."

"Fine. Tonight." I opened the door and stepped outside. He stepped out right behind me, so close I could feel his warmth on my back.

"In your cottage," he said, low and in my ear.

"That's fine." I smiled at Adeline, who was wearing a

coat that swallowed up her pregnant belly. "Come by, but you better bring me wine."

"Joss." Adeline walked toward me with open arms. I wrapped my arms around her as best I could without squeezing her belly. "You made it."

"Of course I did." I pulled away, setting my hands on her bump and smiling. "You've grown so much in just two weeks."

"I know. My feet know it, too." Addie sighed. "I was just telling Eli that I don't think I can sleep upstairs. Just thinking about stairs makes me winded."

"I already told Yarra to set up the cottage for us," Elias said behind her. I instantly let go of Addie's bump and dropped into a small curtsy to greet him. He rolled his eyes. "No one is around, Joslyn. You don't have to do that right now."

"We all have to do it, brother," Aramis said, bowing before stepping in closer.

"Aramis is right. All of us need to do it whether or not people are around. It's the only way we won't forget to when they are. Besides, you're the King and Queen. You need to learn to stop acting like commoners," their mother said.

Adeline turned her back and rolled her eyes as she looked at me. I bit my lip to keep from laughing.

"The year is 2020, Mother," Pilar said, walking over and giving me a hug, followed by her fiancé Benjamin Drake. "I'm freezing my butt off. Where are the carts?"

"They should be here soon," Elias said.

"You were the one who forced us to come outside so that you could point out dead flowers," Benjamin said, shaking his head. "As if you're not responsible for killing all of our plants."

"First of all, your ex-fiancée gave me two orchids in the middle of winter, so if anything, we need to blame her for this," Pilar said. "It's not my fault I don't have a green thumb."

"Can we just get back inside while we wait?" the Queen Mother said. "It really is unpleasantly cold today."

"They say we may get a storm this weekend," Ben added.

"A snowstorm?" Addie asked, gasping.

"Don't worry. All of the cottages have generators," Eli said. "And we have everything we need in them."

It was true. Eli made it a point to build the cottages as small apartments, equipped with kitchens, bathrooms, guest areas, and bedrooms. Add to that the service people who were constantly around to clean and bring food, it was like staying at one of the best resorts. As we walked inside, Addie informed us that we'd be given an itinerary of events while we were here. It was nothing major, she said, but the list would serve as something we could use so that we don't stay cooped up in our respective cottages and actually spend time together, which was what this holiday was supposed to be for. Because it was Christmas, we'd brought along wrapped presents that were being deposited beneath one of the trees in the palace.

"We're going to decorate the tree together tonight," Addie said. "So after we take a rest, we'll have dinner together and meet in the library, which is where our tree will be."

"Why aren't we opening presents beneath the tree in the entrance?" the Queen Mother asked. "Or in the Hall of Mirrors? That's the biggest tree of all."

"The library is cozier, Mother," Elias said, putting an arm around Addie. "We decided that would be the best place to relax and have drinks while we decorated and listened to music."

I smiled. This was beginning to sound like a real holiday now.

"When is David coming?" Pilar asked. "I texted him but he hasn't responded."

"He's probably still on his flight," I said. "He's on his way to Spain, then London, then he'll be here Friday evening."

I wasn't sure why, but I looked at Aramis after I responded to her and found him staring at me with an unreadable expression on his face. He looked upset. Maybe he was still thinking about the list and being forced to date someone, anyone, to save face. Maybe he was thinking about something else entirely. Regardless of what was on his mind, the look on his face made my heart do a little flip and for the millionth time today I had to remind myself that contract or no contract, Prince Aramis was not for me.

CHAPTER FOUR

'D JUST FINISHED SHOWERING WHEN I HEARD THE KNOCK ON the door. With a towel wrapped around myself and my hair dripping, I walked over and pulled it open. There were no peepholes on the doors, but I figured it had to be Pilar or Adeline. Instead, I found myself looking into Aramis's dangerously seductive gaze as he took in my attire. I held the towel tighter and cleared my throat.

"What do you want?"

"I thought you'd be ready by now. I was going to walk to the main house with you." He glanced in that direction briefly, then back at me. "I forgot to bring the wine, but it seemed futile since we have to go over there anyway."

"Oh." I eyed him up and down. He was wearing trousers, boots, and a button-down underneath a heavy black coat. "I just need a minute."

"Your hair is wet and it's cold out. You need more than a minute."

"Okay?"

"Well, are you going to invite me in?" He arched an eyebrow.

"I'm naked."

"Are you inviting me to take advantage of this fact?" He began to smile but stopped when he saw how unprepared for all of this I was. "I'm kidding, Joslyn. I can wait in the sitting area while you change."

"Oh. Yes. Of course." I shook my head and stepped away from the door, shivering as soon as I was out of the line of the wind. It really was cold out. "Just . . . watch television or something."

I disappeared into the bathroom and closed the door behind me. The closet shared a space with the bathroom, which made it clear that Aramis had been joking about seeing me naked. Sometimes, it felt like it was all he ever did. He'd always been humorous and a flirt, but these days it seemed like he hid his uncertainties behind his jokes as well. Once I was dressed, wearing jeans, a camisole, and a loose ivory sweater over it, I picked up my brown booties and walked back out into the sitting area where he was, sitting across from him on the other couch.

"Did you get a chance to look at the list I sent you?"

"Yes, and I'm not interested."

"In any of them?" I set my foot down with a thump. "There were twelve women on that list."

"Twelve women. I've met more than half of them. I went to school with three. Trust me, they're not interesting."

"What in the world makes a woman interesting to you, Aramis?"

"Lots of things." He shrugged a shoulder.

"Like what? List something." I sighed, shaking my head. "You know what? You're going to tell me what you're looking for and that's where I'm going to start and before you tell me you don't want to look at all, I'll kindly remind you that your mother is going to start inviting women over with or without your input."

"Fine."

We both stood up, I grabbed my coat, and we walked outside, heading in the direction of the palace. The gardens were lit and beautiful. Every time I was here, I couldn't help but to think about the past and all of the things that this lush grass had seen. Aramis and Elias had thrown parties here and those had gotten out of hand some of the time, but I'd always left before the real trouble started. The few times I didn't leave early, I'd ended up in Aramis's arms. I bit my lip and glanced away as I thought about that. I'd lost my virginity to him and slept with him two more times after that. It was something I didn't regret, not by a long shot, but I definitely tried not to think about it much. All those years ago, a part of me thought I'd be the one to tame him. Now I realized that would never be the case. Men like Aramis couldn't be tamed and there was no use in trying.

CHAPTER FIVE

ARAMIS

SHE'D ASKED ME TO LIST THE THINGS I WAS LOOKING FOR IN a woman and I kept coming up blank. I wouldn't admit it aloud, but I'd never given it much thought. I always figured when I met the woman for me, I'd know. How would I know? Well, I wasn't sure. A spark? Some kind of flashing lights going off that would alert me that I finally found her? I knew all of that was far-fetched, of course, but I couldn't seem to help myself. I wanted it to be blatantly obvious that I'd found the one. I didn't want to be stuck in a loveless marriage like my parents. Of course, my mother would never say all of the years she spent married to my father had been loveless. She wouldn't admit it aloud, but we knew. It was the reason Elias was dead set on marrying a commoner he'd fallen in love with instead of one of the many suitors our mother had in mind for him. It was why Pilar refused to even think about being set up on a date. Instead, she'd left on holiday and found love on a whim, with someone she'd known for years, at that. Sometimes I wondered if that was the key. Maybe I should be looking a little closer to the women around me. The only issue is that the only woman consistently around me was Joslyn and she hated me. More than hated me. She couldn't seem to sit beside me long enough without acting like she was uncomfortable. My mind drifted back to the list she'd given me. I looked over at her as she drank her after-dinner tea. We were the only ones still sitting at the long dinner table. My mother, Adeline, Elias, Pilar, and Ben were all in the next room, decorating the Christmas tree.

"What?" Joslyn side-eyed me as she sipped her tea.

"I'm thinking about the list."

"Oh." She set the cup down. "And?"

"Looks are important."

"Obviously." She rolled her eyes. "It's your list, after all."

"I don't want a doormat. I want a woman who can defend herself."

"From you?" Joslyn arched an eyebrow. "Don't you think that's an issue? That someone would have to defend themselves from their partner all the time?"

"Only in jest. I don't insult people, Joslyn."

"You insult me all the time." She picked her cup back up and continued drinking, blowing between small sips.

"And you like it."

"I do not. Just because I don't cry about it doesn't mean I like it."

"You insult me right back."

"Rightfully so."

"Because you're not a doormat." I arched a brow. "And you can take a joke. That's next on the list: able to take a joke."

"Okay." She smiled behind the cup, her green eyes sparkling. "Anything else, master?"

My blood roared in my ears at the sound of that. I glanced away to hide the lust I knew was written all over my face. I wasn't in love with Joslyn, but there was definitely a spark there. Always had been. A spark I ignored and squandered any chance I got out of respect for her post as Pilar's secretary and now mine. Out of respect for my mother, who continuously reminded me that I couldn't have her. The butler walked into the room and gathered our attention.

"Sir." He bowed at me. "There's someone at the door for you."

"For me?" I frowned, standing up. "I didn't invite anyone."

"It's a gentleman and a . . . " He cleared his throat. "I think you should come to the door."

"Okay." I folded my napkin and tossed it on the table, leaving Joslyn sitting there sipping on her tea as I walked down the long corridors of Versailles.

I took the stairs quickly and walked to the main door, the butler quick at my heels. He rushed past me as we reached the door and opened it. There was an older gentleman on the other side holding the hand of a boy.

"May I help you?" I asked, shooting a look at the butler for him to leave. He did quickly.

"I'm Rudolph. I've waited a long time for this. Had my speech planned out of what I would say when I saw you. Thought I'd knock you straight in the nose, actually, but now that I'm here it doesn't seem worth it."

"Wh . . . I'm sorry, do I know you?" I braced myself, my heart stopping for a moment. I'd been in a car accident and the people in the other car hadn't survived. We'd made sure their family got an adequate compensation, not that any compensation was adequate for the loss of a life, but it was something. Was this man the father of one of the people? The brother? The son? I hadn't asked for specifics.

"No, we've never met." He scoffed. "My daughter Esmée and you are well-acquainted. Or that is, you were some eight years ago. Esmée Laurent."

"I'm sorry, I don't recall an Esmée."

"Of course." He shook his head, scoffing again.

"I'm sorry, what is it you need? Money? Does your daughter need money?"

"You think you can just throw money at us, is that it? For years you've been sending money to Esmée and now you claim you don't know her name."

"What?" I blinked. "What are you talking about?"

"This here is Oscar." He patted the boy's head. "Your son."

I felt myself stumble back, though I wasn't sure if I actually did or if it was the air rushing out of my head so quickly. I looked at the boy again. He had the same complexion as me, the same green eyes, his hair was lighter than mine, but I guessed that could be from his mother's side. Still. I shook my head.

"There's no way."

"You didn't know?" Rudolph blinked. "You've been sending payments."

"Not me." I couldn't stop staring at the boy. He looked scared, like it was taking everything in him not to hide behind the man next to him.

"Grandpa, I want to leave now," the boy said, tugging Rudolph's hand.

"We talked about this." The man looked down at the boy. "You have to be strong."

Years of hearing those words came flooding back to me, but the only thing I could do was stare at the boy, feeling like my heart was going to rip out of my body. Was he really mine? I had no recollection of an Esmée. A few years back there had been a rumor that someone had gotten pregnant by one of us, but my brother and I had looked into it and it had been a made-up story, someone after money. I looked at the man again.

"How do I know you're not lying?"

"I have proof." The man handed over a crumpled folder. I took it tentatively and looked inside. There was a birth certificate with the boy's name—Oscar Aramis Laurent—only the mother's name listed as a parent. Behind that, a paternity test. My heart pounded faster. Someone had taken my DNA and done this without my consent and then kept it from me. Who would do such a thing? I closed the folder and looked at the boy. He looked less than thrilled to be here. I looked at the man again.

"Why now? Why are you here?"

"My daughter, she . . . she's in the hospital." Rudolph's voice wavered. "I've got nowhere else to take him."

"So, you brought him here?"

"There comes a time in life where a man has to stand up and do what's right. I was hoping you'd do that today."

I nodded, swallowed the lump in my throat that had been sitting there during the entirety of this conversation. "What's wrong with his mother? Is she okay?"

"She will be, God willing. She had a fall. Putting up stupid Christmas decorations." Rudolph scowled. "It's what happens when you refuse to let a man into your life. She hasn't wanted to let any man get too close since you . . . you know."

"No, I don't know." It was the truth. I'd never had a

relationship with his daughter. A one-night stand, sure, definitely, according to the paternity test, but not more than that.

"She doesn't trust easily."

"Do you need money for her medical bills?"

"That would help." Rudolph gave a nod. "What I need is for Oscar to stay here for a while. He deserves a father, don't you think?"

I nodded, unable to look at the boy in question. I wasn't big on crying or showing emotion, but somehow I knew if I looked at the boy I'd cry.

"But I don't want to stay here, Poppa."

"You have to." Rudolph crouched down and looked Oscar in the eye. "I'll be back to check on you in two days. You have a phone to call me whenever you want. I'll have your mum call as soon as she can." He stood and looked at me. "I trust you'll take good care of him."

"I will." I swallowed.

I stood with Oscar at the door as his grandfather walked to his car and drove off. We waited until he was out of eyesight but remained unmoved as I cleared my throat.

"I guess you should come inside." I stepped back into the house. "Did you bring your things?"

"I brought this." He picked up a small suitcase. "I didn't pack much."

"That's okay. We can get you whatever you need."

He smiled slightly, but couldn't seem to look at me

or meet my eyes. I didn't blame him. We were strangers. Deeply tied strangers. I didn't know the first thing about children. I was planning on learning when my nephew was born in a couple of months, but as I walked through the palace with Oscar, I knew that had to change now.

"This is big."

"It is big." I smiled.

"Are there ghosts? My mum says there are ghosts here."

"I haven't seen any, but I wouldn't be surprised."

"Will I have to sleep alone? I don't like sleeping alone."

"You can sleep in my cottage. It has three bedrooms. Is that okay?"

"I think so." He was looking at everything as we walked. I had to try to figure out a way to tell my family. They were used to my charades, but a child was something they wouldn't expect. Or maybe they would. Someone obviously knew about Oscar. Someone had been keeping me in the dark all this time. Footsteps rung out as we walked, and Oscar and I slowed down. My heart pounded. I hoped it was a butler or house maid, but braced myself for my brother, my mother, my sister-in-law. It was Joslyn, a confused look on her face when she saw the boy.

"Hello." She frowned, smiling as she closed the distance between us. "Who are you?"

"Oscar."

"Oscar. I'm Joslyn." She shook his hand and looked at me. "And what is Oscar doing here?"

"He's my son."

Joslyn's color drained from her face. "What?"

"My son. His grandfather just dropped him off."

"I . . ." She looked between me and Oscar and back at me. "May I speak to you?"

"Hey, do you mind waiting for us right here?" I asked Oscar. "I'll only be a second."

"That's fine." He shrugged and walked over to the painting beside us as I stepped out of earshot with Joslyn.

"A son?" she whispered. "Why didn't you tell me?"

"I just found out."

"What?"

"I just found out five minutes ago."

"Are you sure he's yours?" Her frown deepened as she looked over at Oscar. "I mean, he looks just like you, but . . . he's . . . how old is he?"

"I don't know."

"You don't know? Who's his mother?"

"I don't know. Some woman named Esmée that I don't recall meeting. A one-night stand the grandfather said."

"Aramis." Joslyn blinked.

"He showed me paternity papers." I waved the crumpled folder. She took it from my hands and looked at it.

"It looks legitimate."

"I know. He says I've been sending money all these years, but I haven't. I couldn't. I didn't know."

"So, who did?" She met my gaze.

"I don't know."

"Elias?"

"Maybe."

"Would he not tell you?"

"My brother is my best friend. I love him to death, but he's the King. Kings keep secrets."

"A son, Aramis." Joslyn's voice was a whisper.

"I know."

"Your family is going to . . . oh my God, we need to tell your mother to sit down."

"We can't warn them. I'm going to tell them and we're going to pay close attention to each person's reaction."

"Okay." She nodded. "Where's his mother now?"

"Hospital."

"Oh my God, is she okay?"

"Her father says she will be. The boy has nowhere else to go."

"Are you happy?"

"Am I happy? I'm too shocked to be happy."

"Okay well, let's get this over with. We'll have to make arrangements for him to sleep in your cottage."

"I already spoke to him about that."

"Good."

"I think maybe you should stay there as well."

"In your cottage?" She frowned up at me. "Why?"

"I don't know what to do with a child, Joslyn. What if I accidentally kill him?"

"He's not a newborn." She laughed. "He looks pretty independent to me."

"Still. Just in case. The last thing we need is a lawsuit on our hands."

"A lawsuit?" She laughed louder. "That's what you're worried about?"

"Please don't leave me alone right now."

Her expression turned serious. "I won't."

CHAPTER SIX

JOSLYN

"A son?" Adeline repeated for the fifth time.

I was grateful I'd had the foresight to ask Pilar's fiancé, Ben, to go outside and hang out with Oscar before Aramis and I walked in to tell the family the news. Oscar seemed giddy to meet a footballer and this way, he wouldn't have to hear the tone in their voices when they were speaking about him. It wasn't the boy's fault that his father was an irresponsible idiot.

"One of you knew about him and I need to know who." Aramis looked at everyone in the room. Everyone except for me. He knew I didn't know. "His mother has been receiving money from me for years."

"And you didn't know he existed?" Adeline gasped, setting a hand over her pregnant belly. "My God."

"Did you know?" Aramis looked at Elias, who shook his head.

"Of course not. I wouldn't keep that from you."

We all looked at the Queen Mother. She'd been the only one to have no reaction to the news. She flattened her lips as she looked at Aramis.

"Someone had to get rid of the scandal."

I felt my mouth drop and looked at Pilar and Adeline to see theirs had also met the same fate.

"How could you keep this from me?" Aramis asked. "A son. Are you kidding me?"

"Why would you do that?" Elias asked.

"We could not handle another scandal. Our family has already been through enough. Our name has been dragged through the mud. Do you think a child would help matters?"

"So we should all pay for our father's sins?" Aramis's voice boomed throughout the room. "It's one thing to keep the public out of our business. It's an entirely different thing to keep us in the dark about children we've fathered!"

"I'm going to be sick." Adeline pressed the hand not on her stomach over her mouth.

"I haven't fathered any children," Elias said, setting a hand on her shoulder.

"How would you know?" Her eyes widened. "Aramis just found out about this."

"Addie. You know me. You know how careful I am. I have not fathered any children." Elias's compassion shined as he looked at his wife, pleading that she believe him.

"I can't believe you did this." Aramis shook his head. "How could you hide a child from me?"

"When was I to tell you? When you were jumping from bed to bed or after you'd done too much cocaine to even show up at events you were supposed to be in?" the Queen Mother asked. "Please enlighten me. The best thing that happened to that child was his mother." She pointed toward the door. "That woman is a saint. I knew it the day I met her, and you would have ruined their lives if you'd decided to be part of it."

Aramis didn't speak. You could hear a pin drop in that room and it terrified me. Was she insinuating that she'd been in contact with Esmée and her grandson all along? Had she visited them? One look at Aramis and I knew he was thinking the same thing. We all were. Elias was the one who cleared his throat and asked.

"Do you have a relationship with the boy?"

"Not a relationship, but I have visited."

"Jesus." Aramis shut his eyes and shook his head. When he opened them again the fight had worn out of him. He looked sad. "Here I was willing to sacrifice my social life for you. Going over a list of women to settle down with and all along you were hiding this? You disgust me." He spoke to his mother directly. I held my breath.

"I was doing the right thing for our family." The Queen Mother's voice broke.

"Don't do me any more favors," Aramis spat out as he made his way to the door, leaving and shutting it so loudly behind him that the glass sconces on either side rattled.

"I can't believe you did that," Pilar whispered.

"I did it—"

"For the family, yes, you've said, but that doesn't make it right." Pilar shook her head. "Aramis has been through a lot. He doesn't deserve this."

"Where's the boy now?" Adeline asked.

"Outside with Ben. And Aramis now, I'm sure. His grandfather dropped him off," I said. "His mother is in the hospital and the grandfather didn't have anyone else to turn to."

"I want to meet him." Elias began walking toward the doors.

"Maybe you should let them have their moment, love," Adeline said, walking quickly toward him and setting a hand on his arm.

"But he's my nephew." Elias frowned.

"And he's your brother's son. Don't you think they need some time?"

"I think he'd like to meet you," I said, nodding at Adeline when she looked at me. She let go of his arm and Elias left the room, shutting the door much quieter than his brother had.

"He's going to hate me." The Queen Mother sat down, bringing a hand over her mouth.

"With good reason," Pilar said, shaking her head and leaving the room. She didn't bother closing the door.

Adeline and I looked at each other. We were the only ones left with the enemy and I wasn't sure how she felt, but I wasn't comfortable staying, so I began to walk toward the door. Adeline followed. We also left the door open behind us as we made our way out.

"Where are they?" she asked.

"I have no idea. They were here when I went inside."

"What's he like? The boy? What's his name?"

"Oscar. He's adorable. Around six or seven. He seems well-mannered."

"I can't believe Aramis has a son," she whispered.

"Me neither."

"How do you feel about it?"

"Me?" I frowned, slowing my steps as we neared the hall of mirrors, where the men and boy were laughing.

"Yes, you." Adeline shot me a pointed look.

"I don't feel any kind of way. I guess I'm just hoping this doesn't make him spiral out of control."

"Please, Joss. I know you better than anyone. I've seen the look on your face every time their mother asks you to find a match for Aramis."

"You mean the look of terror because I know that no woman will ever put up with him?"

"I mean the look of jealousy because you like him." She pursed her lips as we stopped by the open door, looking inside.

They were playing with a football. Who knows where they'd gotten it from, but I could think of thirty things that could go wrong with a football in this room. None of them seemed to care though. Elias, the King, was the one heading the game, after all. Aramis and his son were side by side and Ben was next to Elias, who had the ball at his feet. Pilar was taking her heels off, seemingly ready to join the match.

"They look so happy," Adeline said, and I could hear the smile in her voice.

They did look happy. They'd met Oscar not even ten minutes ago and had fully accepted him as theirs. It was how they were. Even Aramis, as much of a pain in the ass as he was. As I stood there watching him smile at his son with a kind of wonderous look in his eyes I'd never seen before, I felt my heart break a little more.

CHAPTER SEVEN

A LOT HAD HAPPENED IN THE FOUR DAYS FOLLOWING OSCAR'S arrival. My things were moved to Aramis's three-bedroom cottage, where each of us had our own room, but shared the common area of the small kitchen and living room. Aramis and Oscar were gone most of the time, father-son bonding that neither one of them had experienced before. It was nice to see him so comfortable in his new role and paying attention to something other than droves of women. I'd been busy helping Adeline with Christmas decorations and things for the nursery here—a room the baby wouldn't be using often, as they didn't live in Versailles, and was completely unnecessary, but who was going to say no to the King? Not me. Elias wanted the baby to have a room in each of their homes, regardless of how often they visited.

Four days of baby talk, seeing Aramis with a small version of himself, and being the third wheel to Pilar and Benjamin's walks in the garden. I'd gotten used to hanging out with the two of them, but somehow I actually felt like a third wheel now. Maybe it was because I'd been on a few dates with David, Ben's best friend and personal assistant, and in that case I hadn't been the third wheel. Those had been double dates. The thought of David gave me pause. He was supposed to visit this weekend. Supposed to, that is, until he called last night and said his trip would be a quick twenty-four-hour one instead of the entire weekend. I supposed it was fine. At least I'd have twenty-four hours of doing something other than tending to my friends and their partners or their children. I didn't mind doing it, of course not, it was my job, after all. How many people could say they worked with their best friends? Not many, I supposed. How many people could say they enjoyed what they did for a living? Again, not many. I always kept those two points in the forefront of my mind, as to not forget. Some days, it was difficult. Some days, even though they'd always treated me like I was part of their family, I missed my own. I missed my mother and father and even my little brother, who I didn't always get along with, but always understood me. Today was that day. I just felt lonely. So, even if David wasn't coming for a full weekend, I was really looking forward to seeing him later.

"Someone looks happy today."

I turned to see Aramis and Oscar walking toward me. They were both wearing camouflage gear. Today, unlike every other day since we'd been here, the sun was out and there was a peculiar warmth to the winter. Aramis was smiling, waiting for me to respond.

"I am. David is coming later."

"Right. David." He rolled his eyes, but kept his smile. "Where will he stay? Your old cottage?"

"I guess so. I'll probably be staying with him." I tore my gaze from his and looked at Oscar. "How are you doing today? Having fun?"

"We're going fishing."

"Were going fishing," Aramis corrected. "Unfortunately, the frozen pond didn't get the memo."

I laughed. "So where are you off to now?"

"We're grabbing lunch and going to visit his mother."

"Oh." I blinked. "Is she doing better?"

"It seems so. She wants to see Oscar." Aramis put a hand on the boy's shoulder. "And I'm sure he's dying to see his mother as well."

Oscar smiled wide, nodding. "But I want to stay here longer."

"We'll come right back here." Aramis smiled down at him. "Do you want to let Madame Contessa know that we're hungry and need food?"

"Yes." Oscar shimmied out of his father's hold and ran toward the palace as we watched.

"Don't you think it's dangerous to let him roam around alone?"

"I used to." Aramis was frowning when I looked back at him. "Besides, there's staff in every corner right now. Elias had someone set up every ten feet so Oscar won't get lost."

I felt my brows raise. It never failed to amaze me that they could just request something like that done with a snap of a finger.

"At what time is David due?"

"He should be here in an hour." I glanced at the watch on my right wrist and saw that it was already noon.

"Are you picking him up at the airport or sending for him?"

"Sending for him. Why?"

"Just curious." Aramis smiled, that tilt of one side of his lip he did, and shrugged a shoulder and I knew there was more to his statement.

"What?"

"It's just, when people are in love they try to spend every moment they can with their partner. They don't send drivers to pick them up at airports."

"What do you know about love?" I raised an eyebrow, then corrected, "Romantic love anyway."

"I know a little." He stepped forward and for the first time in a long time, I fought the urge to step back, my heart fluttering into my throat. "How much do you know? Are you in love with him?"

"Maybe."

"That sounds like a no." He raised an eyebrow.

"Like a no." I laughed, shaking my head. "Really, Aramis?"

"Really."

"I don't know why you would assume anything. You've never seen us together."

"You're right." He stepped closer still.

I wished he wasn't looking at me so intently, those dark green eyes casing mine like I was the one he was hunting today. I felt trapped even though I could back away, I could walk away. My heart was in my throat though, and I couldn't move, not when he was looking at me like that. Not when he was stepping into me like that. Not when we were near the same spot he'd done this to me so many years ago, the night he'd offered me his hand. The night I'd caved and taken it, letting him lead me away from here. The night I'd given him my virginity, because I couldn't think of anyone more perfect to lose it to, despite knowing he'd never be mine.

"I've been thinking about that night a lot lately," he said, and then I did step back slightly, eyes wide, heart pounding.

"What about it?"

"I wish I'd been a different man then. I wish I'd paid more attention to what was in front of me."

"You had years to remedy that and didn't." I chuckled lightly. I'd had years to come to terms with the fact that he didn't see me like that and that was fine. I knew it wasn't a me thing, it was an Aramis thing.

"What if I want to remedy it now?"

"What are you saying?"

"Why don't you put yourself on the list and erase everyone else?"

"What makes you think I would want that?"

"You want me. I know you want me."

"You think everyone who breathes the same air as you wants you." I shook my head, glancing away.

"Are you telling me you don't?" He brought a hand toward me and grabbed mine.

My heart ricocheted in my chest. It was déjà vu. It was a mirror. Why did I feel like I had then, grasping at straws, gasping for air? I was a woman now. Experienced. I yanked my hand from his grasp.

"Please stop. I have a boyfriend. He's coming to visit. You have a son that you're dedicating all of your time to, as you should be, and well, there's the contract. We can't do this. Not now." I swallowed.

Not ever would have been more apt, but I knew how to speak to Aramis to get him to back off, and concrete, definitive things existed only for him to tear down. He stepped away with a nod, and walked away without another word. I could tell he was brewing, but wasn't he always? On my walk to meet Adeline in the library to decorate some more, I couldn't shake the conversation. I couldn't shake the feeling that overcame me because of it, things I hadn't felt in years, not since my college boyfriend whom everyone including myself thought I would marry. Until we found out he was a lying cheater, that was. I pushed my thoughts aside as I opened the door and walked inside, smiling at the sight of a very pregnant Adeline standing in the middle of the room with a confused look on her face.

"What? Did you decide another Christmas tree was too much?" I asked.

"Very funny." She glanced over at me, placing her hand on her belly. "The baby hasn't stopped moving all day. I'm beginning to think he either really hates this holiday or wants to come sooner to celebrate it with us."

I laughed, walking over and placing my hands on her belly, feeling him kick. "And what do you want?"

"I would love to have him in my arms already, but I don't think I want him sleeping in the nursery in here." She met my eyes. "I'm afraid it's haunted."

"I don't doubt that it is." I let go of her stomach and looked at everything she had laid out on the table. "I'm afraid to ask who helped you do all of this."

"It wasn't heavy."

"You say that about everything, Addie. You need to be careful." I shot her a look.

"I know. I just hate feeling like I can't do anything."

"You have a full staff that wants to help. Genuinely wants to help. They're all so excited about the baby. Let them do their jobs." I tried for a comforting smile.

I knew Addie better than anyone and knew how much

she hated to have a full staff. She'd come a long way and had certainly gotten used to it, but it was still too much to ask for help when it came to mundane things like carrying a box.

"What's up?"

"What?" I blinked.

"What's up? You look like you've got a lot on your mind."

"Do I?" I frowned. "Nothing. I mean, David is coming into town, so I guess my mind is elsewhere."

"That'll be fun." She grinned. "Are you two getting serious?"

"I don't know."

"You don't know?" She set down the ribbon in her hand and made her way to the sitting area. I followed and sat beside her on the couch. "Let's talk. I feel like it's been ages since we've caught up, just the two of us." She slipped her shoes off and put her feet on the coffee table as she waited, then said, "You like him."

"I do like him. What's not to like?" I said with a laugh. "He's handsome, sexy, passionate about a job he does well in."

"He helps celebrities in crisis, right? That's what he does?"

"Basically. With Ben, he helped him clean up his reputation."

"So essentially, what you're doing with Aramis."

"More or less." I tilted my head as I thought about it.

"Except I'm trying to find Aramis a good woman to settle down with."

"Still? Even with this new development and Oscar?" Adeline sounded surprised.

"The Queen Mother still wants him to have a wife."

"I'm sure he doesn't want anything to do with her wishes right now." She scowled. "Besides, my husband is the King and he calls the shots now. We think that particular issue should be put aside for now."

"I agree."

"Good."

"Have you decided on a name?"

"Elias wants to name him after his father, but I can't imagine why. His father was not very well loved." She pursed her lips.

"What do you want to name him?"

"Alexander."

"That's a nice, strong name."

"Isn't it?" She shrugged a shoulder. "Eli doesn't like it."

"What names does he like?"

"Louis, Charles, Henry, Philip."

"Boring names."

"So boring." Adeline laughed loudly. "But I guess the future king's name doesn't have to be fun."

"And you can give him thirteen names if you really wanted. I'm sure you can slide one in there that you don't mind calling him."

"Very true." She laughed.

"Where is Elias now? I don't think I've seen him leave your side in months."

"Meeting with my father and some other members of Parliament."

"Speaking of boring."

"Exactly. The only fun thing going on in there are the croissants and hot cocoa Elias decided to provide them with today. I think they're discussing city planning and street building. All of the things citizens love to complain about but have no solutions for."

"Well, I hope they discuss a way to rid us of traffic. God knows it's been awful these days."

"You live two blocks from Aramis. It takes you two minutes to get to work." Addie shot me an amused look.

"It took me hours to get all of the Christmas party things together when I was driving all across town. Besides, you know how Aramis refuses to drive after the accident? He fired his driver and has called me no less than ten times in one week to drive him places."

"Aramis fired Ahmed? When?"

"Who knows. He says he showed up to work late one day."

Adeline laughed lightly, then a little harder.

"What's so funny?"

"Ahmed was not fired."

"What do you mean?"

"He's been driving around for us for a month now. Aramis told us he got a new, temporary driver."

"Meaning me." I blinked. "Why would he do that?"

"Why would he not?" Addie's eyes twinkled. "He likes you. You know that."

"He doesn't like me. He doesn't like anyone."

"He definitely likes you, Joss. He spends most of his days either asking where you are or trying to figure out how to spend time with you."

He'd never outright told me he liked me. I said this aloud, to which Adeline's response was a small shrug.

"He thinks you hate him. Why would he tell you he likes you?"

"I don't hate him." I felt myself frown.

"It doesn't matter how you feel if your actions show the opposite."

I thought of our earlier conversation. He'd always flirted with me, but Aramis was a serial flirt. I never took it to heart because there was no point in it. If that was the case, if I knew that, why in the world was my heart pounding as hard as it was?

CHAPTER EIGHT

ARAMIS

I DIDN'T LIKE DAVID.

He didn't seem like a bad guy on paper. It was his job to help people get their shit together and I knew that showed some form of decency. He'd helped my soon-to-be brother-in-law Ben get his shit together when he needed it. I didn't like the way he looked at Joss or the way he didn't let her finish her sentences before jumping in with his own ideas. She had her own ideas and they were better than his as far as I was concerned.

"Joss tells me she paused the matchmaking," David said from across the dinner table.

"It is paused," I said, taking a sip of wine.

We'd already had dinner and were now finishing up the wine. Oscar had gone to bed early with his new nanny, the daughter of the cook here who needed a holiday job. She was young, but Oscar took an immediate liking to her, and so, when she offered to play with him and put him to bed so that I could enjoy dinner with my family, I agreed.

"Any particular reason?" David asked. "I have quite a few women I think would be suitable for you."

"I'm not interested at the moment, but thank you. Besides, Joslyn has all of that sorted out for me. I don't think she needs outside help."

"Considering you've been at this for a year now and still haven't found anyone, I would consider a little outside help."

I looked at Joss, who was taking a big gulp of wine, clearly trying to hide her discomfort, and decided I definitely did not like David. Joss never held back her thoughts, not when I pushed her like this. Had I made that remark, Joss would have ripped my head off. Why was she giving this creep special treatment? I waited to see if she was going to say anything. Instead, she let him continue speaking.

"My offer stands. If you want my help, I'd be glad to provide it for you," he said.

"For a price, I'm sure," Elias added.

"A small fee if I match him with the right woman," David said. "If it doesn't work, it doesn't work."

"You're that confident that you can find someone for him?" Pilar asked.

I shot my sister a glare. Not only was she now more invested than ever in my finding a girlfriend, but she'd been the one to connect David with Joslyn. I loved my sister, but right now I was not her biggest fan.

"Maybe you should give it a shot," Ben added beside her.

"I think Aramis has enough on his plate," Adeline said and I'd never been more grateful for my sister-in-law.

"I do have enough on my plate." I shot each of them a pointed look.

"You have free time." Pilar shrugged a shoulder.

"I'll tell you what, why don't I invite someone over tonight?" David said, pulling out his phone. "I know the perfect person. She's an aristocrat, is on holiday nearby, she's smart, funny, and a knockout."

"In that case, why don't you have a go at her?" I raised an eyebrow.

"I'm satisfied at the moment," he said, not even bothering to look up from his phone.

Joss blushed beside him. I shot her a glare. How dare she feel things for this asshole? I mean, really. I knew I was an asshole a lot of the time, but I wasn't this. She would have been better off with one of my best friends from college than this guy. At least they'd grown up and realized their shit stank.

"What do you think, Joslyn?"

"Me?" She blinked, seemingly surprised that I'd ask her for her opinion at all. God, I'd messed up with this girl. "I think you might as well give it a shot."

"Fine."

"It's settled. Does 9 p.m. work?" He looked at me, then at Elias, and back at me.

"9 p.m. is fine. Give me her details so we can inform the gatekeeper," Elias said.

"9 p.m. is my bedtime, but now I have to try to stay up to at least catch a glimpse of this aristocratic beauty," Adeline said.

"There is no one in the world as beautiful as you, my Queen." Elias kissed the top of his wife's head. "But I'm curious myself. We should know her if she's from a prominent family."

"She's Greek," David said. "She recently purchased a bungalow out here to get away."

"You seem to know a lot about her." Pilar's eyes narrowed slightly. Finally, someone with a brain.

"Not intimately, if that's what you're assuming." David chuckled.

And with that, we all finished our wine and decided to meet back in this room when our guest arrived.

CHAPTER NINE

Her name was Cassandra Mountbatten and she checked off every single box, not that David let me be the judge of that. Saying he was my boyfriend was a bit much, but we had gone on a handful of amazing dates, so the way he was acting here, in front of my friends, my bosses, was surprising to me. He'd completely hijacked my job over dinner and as if that wasn't enough he'd been right about the woman. She was everything Aramis wanted. I wasn't sure why I was so annoyed by all of it, but I was.

"You approve?" Aramis asked beside me.

"She checks off all the boxes." I shrugged a shoulder.

"Yet you don't like her."

"What makes you say that?" I glanced up at him. The way he was looking at me made me feel like he could read every single one of my thoughts.

"Your tone. The way you're looking at her like she's wearing last season's Gucci's."

At that, I laughed lightly. "They are definitely this season's."

"Ah, so maybe you're jealous."

"Of her Gucci's?"

"Of her. The idea of her being perfect for me."

"You're crazy." I laughed again, shaking my head. "Did you forget I've been looking for your perfect match for quite some time?"

"Be careful what you wish for. Isn't that what they say?"

"Like I said, you're crazy." I tried to stand my ground, staring him right in the eyes as I said the words, but it seemed futile. He wasn't wrong and I didn't understand why.

"It wouldn't be the first time I've been called crazy." He arched an eyebrow, taking the last sip of wine left in his glass before handing it to me as if I was some sort of butler. "And it wouldn't be the last time I'm not wrong."

I watched as he walked over to Cassandra. Watched as her face lit up at his approach. Watched as they spoke, laughing alongside David, my stomach churning with each flirtatious smile she threw in Aramis's direction. It didn't matter that her hand idly moved toward David when she spoke. It didn't matter that they were standing close to each other. The only thing I could seem to focus on was Aramis's attention on her and what may come of it. I hated it. Setting the glasses in my hand down on the table beside me, I left the room and walked out of the main palace, toward the cottages. When I reached them, I hesitated, unsure if to go to my old one, which I was sharing with David tonight, or Aramis's, where Oscar and his new babysitter were probably watching a movie before bed. There was a second of hesitation on my part before I walked into theirs. Rose turned her attention to the door.

"You're back early." She smiled from the couch, where she was sitting beside Oscar.

"The festivities weren't as fun as I'd envisioned." I took off my scarf, coat, and gloves, and set everything down by the door as I slid my booties off quickly. "How was he?"

"Amazing. As usual." Rose stood. Oscar protested, looking up at her. "I have to go, little man. I'll see you tomorrow, yeah?"

"Will you take me to the stables then?"

"Sure, but I already told you, we need to ask your father for permission to ride."

"But your papa handles the horses. He knows what he's doing."

"He does, but we still need permission." Rose ruffled his hair and walked over to me, picking up her coat along the way.

"May I ride a horse tomorrow?" Oscar asked, looking at me.

"We'll see. We have to ask your father." I smiled as I approached and took the seat Rose vacated, waving at her as she left the cottage.

"But surely you can give permission. He asks you for advice on everything."

"Surely I cannot. Everything regarding your safety is up to your mother and father." I let myself melt into the soft cushions of the couch. Oscar shimmied closer to me. A lump formed in my throat, thinking about his mother, who should be the one cuddling up to him, as I put an arm around him.

"Do you think my mother will be okay?"

"Of course." I squeezed him a little. "She'll be back on her feet before you know it."

"When I saw her she was still not on her feet."

"These things take time." I ran my hand softly through his curls. "You know, your father was in an accident and it took him months to get back to normal."

"Yeah, he told me." He didn't seem convinced as I pulled away slightly so he'd look me in the eyes.

"I'll tell you a secret."

"What?"

"Women are much stronger than men. I have no doubt your mother will have a faster recovery than Aramis. She has you to get back to, after all, but we can't rush her. We need to be patient and trust the doctors."

"Okay." He settled back into my side with a yawn.

"Do you want to turn off the movie?"

"No."

"But you're falling asleep."

"I don't want to go to my own bed and be by myself."

"In that case, we need a blanket." I reached over and grabbed the one beside me, throwing it over the two of us. Oscar yawned again.

"When's Dad coming back?"

"I'm not sure." I bit my lip.

"Why didn't you stay with him?"

"He's meeting with someone. I didn't want to interrupt."

"A woman?"

"What makes you say that?" I felt myself smile. Not much escaped Oscar.

"I heard grandmother talking about him needing a suitor."

"Right. Well, yes, a woman."

Oscar yawned. "Maybe you can be the suitor."

"I don't think so." I laughed. "Let's watch the movie. I'm sure he'll be back before you know it."

CHAPTER TEN

ARAMIS

WAS SURPRISED TO FIND JOSLYN IN ROSE'S PLACE WHEN I GOT back to the cottage. I stood beside the couch, taking off my gloves and scarf as I looked at her and Oscar, sleeping soundly on the couch. My heart skipped a beat. I moved as slowly as I could, lifting Oscar into my arms without waking Joslyn. Once he was safely tucked in bed, I went back for Joslyn, lifting her up the same way. I paused between her bedroom and mine, but when I looked at her sleeping face I made a decision. She'd scream at me in the morning. I knew she would. I didn't care, I wanted her in my bed, even if it was just to sleep soundly beside me. I'd made up my mind tonight. Cassandra was perfect—on paper she was everything I'd said I would settle down with—but she wasn't Joslyn, and despite everything, Joslyn was the one I wanted. She was the one I'd always wanted. I just needed to convince her that we were right together.

CHAPTER ELEVEN

JOSLYN

WOKE UP AT SOME POINT IN THE MIDDLE OF THE NIGHT AND noticed rather quickly that Aramis was sound asleep beside me and I was in his bed. As I sat up and rubbed my eyes looking around, he groaned and stretched out, reaching for me. My heart launched to my throat as his arm wrapped around my waist. I looked down and stared at it, unable to move. I should have. I should have wanted to push it away and run out of there, but somehow, I couldn't bring myself to do it. When I was a teenager, this would have been my dream, having Aramis wanting me to stay in his bed, but I was no longer a teenager. I no longer saw the world through rose-colored glasses. Too many things had happened in the years between our experience together and now. Besides that, his timing was awful. Somewhere on the premises, David was probably looking for me. Though, if last night was any indication, he was probably somewhere with Cassandra of Greece, charmed by her wits and beauty. My eyes rolled at that. Finally, I moved Aramis's arm and got out of bed, picking up my coat and purse along the way. I walked out quietly and peeked inside Oscar's room, where he was still sleeping soundly, before leaving the cottage.

As I shut the door quietly behind me, I put a hand up to shield from the sun and looked to my right to see David walking out of my own cottage. The judgment his expression cast rivaled the sun's rays behind him. I walked over to him, fighting the guilt that weighed me down with each step. I'd done nothing wrong. Nothing. It looked awful on paper, I knew that, but still.

"Hey." I cleared my throat.

"Have a good night?" He raised an eyebrow.

"It's not what it looks like." I sidestepped him and walked into my cottage, beelining toward the restroom. To my surprise, he followed.

"What is it then?"

"It was nothing." I met his gaze in the mirror as I brushed my teeth.

I definitely wasn't going to pee in front of the man. I'd only been seeing him casually for a month. Things like that were definitely not acceptable yet. I frowned at my own thought. We'd already had sex. Surely peeing in front of someone after you'd had their privates in your face wasn't unacceptable. I shook the thought away as I rinsed my mouth and looked at him again.

"You walked out of another man's cottage in the morning . . . after you invited me to come and spend the night with you . . . and you call it nothing." David said the words slowly. So slowly that even I stumbled upon each punctuation, wondering if it had been nothing.

"It was nothing. I didn't have sex with him or anything."

"So what were you doing in there?" He folded his arms.

"I was . . . " I stopped myself. No one outside this palace knew about Oscar. No one was to know about him until the family deemed it acceptable. Aramis wasn't ready to push the kid into the limelight and I understood why. Whenever the scope of the public was on the family, they were instantly tarnished. It was just another reason to stay behind the scenes and try to fix that. I licked my lips. "I'm not at liberty to say, but I was not with him."

"Okay." David gave a nod. "Even if you weren't, I think we should take a break from whatever this is."

"Whatever this is?" My eyes narrowed. "Dating? You mean us dating?"

"Yes, if that's what you want to call it."

"What would you call it?" I crossed my own arms. "We slept together, we spoke on the phone nearly every night, I introduced you to my friends."

"Who also happen to be my friends, so no introduction was necessary."

"You know what I mean." I paused, blinking. "You tried to take my job from me last night!"

"I did not try to take your job." He uncrossed his arms. "I just so happened to know someone who was perfect for what you were looking for and I stepped in. To help."

"It felt like a takeover."

"Interesting choice of words coming from the person they asked to find a suitable mate for the man she spent the night with."

"I already told you . . . " I lowered my voice and uncrossed my own arms. "I already told you that I did not spend the night with him. Not like that."

There was a clearing of throat behind me. I felt a presence and turned around to find Cassandra standing there, a deep blush on her face as she bit her lip. She glanced at me, then at David.

"I'm so sorry. I have to get going. It was a pleasure to meet you, Joslyn." She smiled small and walked toward the front of the cottage quickly.

I let the realization of what had just occurred wash over me, let the sound of the door closing register, and finally turned around to look at David.

"Seriously?"

"She spent the night, but we did not sleep together." He shrugged.

"Get the fuck out."

"Oh, now you want to kick me—"

"Get out," I yelled at the top of my lungs.

I could no longer hold back all of the emotions that were running rampant inside of me—the confusion, the mortification, the anger. David seemed to read all of this correctly, because he walked out quickly without another word. I shut my eyes and gripped the edge of the bathroom counter, counting my breaths 1. 2. 3. 4. 5. 6. 7. 8. 9. 10. And again. 1. 2. 3. 4. 5. 6. 7. 8. 9. 10. I did this two more times, until I knew for certain I'd calmed down, and once I did, I undressed, showered, put on the pajamas I hadn't worn last night, and slunk into bed.

CHAPTER TWELVE

ARAMIS

"WHERE'S JOSLYN?"

"How should I know?" I looked over at Adeline.

"Her cottage is next to yours. I thought maybe you'd seen her."

"Oh." I shook my head, dunking the fresh croissant in my hand into my hot chocolate. "I haven't seen her since last night."

"Maybe she's with David," Elias said.

"Not a chance," Pilar answered. "David left half an hour ago. He looked upset."

"He was upset," Ben said beside her. "I guess they had a spat."

"What kind of spat?" Adeline asked, frowning.

"The kind that leaves people upset." Ben shrugged. "I didn't ask."

"How could you not ask?" Pilar looked aghast.

"Not everyone is nosey." Ben winked at her. She jabbed him in the ribs. "Ouch."

"You deserved it," I said, shrugging. "Everyone is nosey, especially at this table. You should know that by now."

"Do you know what happened?" he asked.

"No idea."

"Hm." Ben's long stare made me wonder how much he was keeping from us on the matter.

I wondered if I'd been the reason for the fight. The thought made me smile a bit. I didn't want Joslyn to be hurt by anyone, but I definitely wanted that relationship to be over sooner rather than later. Her being with David meant she couldn't entertain the idea of being with me. When I finished my breakfast, I looked over at Oscar's nanny, Rose, and told her to take him around the gardens for a little while, and proceeded to plate some breakfast.

"Who is that for?" Elias asked.

"Joslyn."

"You're taking her breakfast?" Adeline's eyes widened.

"I'm impressed at the fact that he can serve his own breakfast." Pilar grinned, then laughed when I lifted my middle finger to her.

"I might as well take her something to eat. I don't

want her moping and complaining and then getting hangry on top of it," I said.

"You sure that's it?" Eli's brow raised.

He looked completely amused by this. My jaw twitched. Normally, I wasn't one to hide things from my brother, but this felt like something I had to keep to myself for the time being, until I was certain that it was even a possibility. Besides, they weren't wrong. I wasn't one to plate my own food, let alone plate it for someone else.

"Will Joss be okay?" That was Oscar, brows pulled in, green eyes concerned.

"She'll be fine, buddy." I shot him a smile. "We'll meet up with you later in the stables. How does that sound?"

"Will we be able to ride?" He perked up in his chair.

"Sure. This is probably the best weather we'll be getting while we're here." I patted his hair and he went back to his croissant.

"Good luck, Romeo," that was what Ben called out when I was leaving the room, as all of them laughed. I shook my head but couldn't help my smile. My family was ridiculous.

As I reached Joslyn's cottage, I took a deep breath and braced myself. I wasn't really sure what I was walking into. Would she be mad I was here? Would she be sad about her riff with David? Would she be crying? God, I hoped she wasn't crying. I'd never been good at dealing with tears and sadness. We were taught to compartmentalize our feelings and push them as far away as possible. Perks of being a royal in a country where everyone was ready to move on from monarchy. I knocked on the door twice before checking to see if it was locked. It wasn't. I let myself in. I was already bringing her food. She couldn't possibly expect me to stand outside with it.

"I was just coming to open it." Joslyn appeared in the living room wearing a long-sleeve, oversized white and blue shirt.

A pajama. It looked like one of my dress shirts, but I could tell it was much softer by the way she grabbed on to the sleeves.

"I brought you breakfast." I walked over to the small table in the kitchenette and set it down.

"Oh." She didn't move from her place between the living room and bedroom. She looked at me, then the plate, then me again. "Thank you."

"Are you not feeling well?"

"I feel fine. Why?" She walked over and sat down.

I sat across from her. It was a two-person table, small and cramped and I hated it. These quarters had been used by palace employees for years before Elias decided to revamp them and turn them into nicer guest suites. As kids we would complain about sleeping in Versailles. The three of us said it was haunted and scary, and it still felt that way to me. For all the work they did on them, they didn't take away any of the eerie feeling. At least now, they were open spaces and light and airy. Before they were remade, they were small and dark. People just assumed my father didn't give a damn about anyone's comfort but himself. I tried to brush that off as an exaggeration, but I wasn't quite sure. The truth was probably somewhere in the middle, in that crevice truth liked to nestle.

"Did Addie send this?" Joss asked, taking a bite of the croissant.

"No."

"Pilar?"

"No."

She frowned, chewing on the soft bread and taking a sip of the hot chocolate I'd also managed to carry over. "Who then?"

"Me."

"Right, but whose idea was it?"

"Mine."

"Yours?" She blinked rapidly. "You decided to bring this for me?"

"Why is that so hard to believe?"

"Why'd you bring it?" Her eyes narrowed slightly as she lowered the half-eaten croissant in her hand.

"Because I was told you didn't feel well."

"Who told you that?"

"Joslyn. Just eat the food and be grateful I brought it." I exhaled, running a hand through my hair.

"I am grateful you brought it, but it's very uncharacteristic for you."

I rolled my eyes. This was exactly why I didn't do nice

things for people. If they'd only accept them and thank me for them, it would be fine, but they always felt the need to discuss it in excess and it bored me. Joslyn continued eating quietly. I took in her appearance. Her eyes weren't red, but they were a little pink. She may have been crying after all.

"Do you want to talk about what happened?"

"With what?" Her eyes shot to mine quickly.

"Okay, let's cut the bullshit. David told Ben he had a fight with you and he left upset, then you didn't show up for breakfast."

"So, you came over here to try to see what gossip I'd tell you so you can go report back to the family. Is that it? Or are you here to make fun of me about it?"

"Jesus, Joslyn. I'm not a monster. I'm here because I want you to eat and I want to make sure you're okay."

"And because you're nosey." She arched an eyebrow as she sipped her hot chocolate.

"And because I'm a little nosey."

She smiled. "We broke up."

"Oh. Are you okay?"

"I'm fine." She side-eyed me as she picked up the thin piece of sausage on her plate. "Though I wish you'd stop looking so smug about my breakup."

"I don't look smug."

"Your eyes smile even when you don't, Aramis." She rolled her eyes. "I will never understand why you get such joy from my relationships failing."

I opened my mouth, then closed it momentarily, my brows pulling in. "I don't get joy from that."

"You do."

"Okay, maybe this time, but not always."

"At least you admit it." She laughed lightly, shaking her head. "Why this time?"

"Because I want you to date me."

"Wh . . . what?" she set everything down and wiped the tips of her fingers with the white cloth napkin on her lap, staring at me like she was trying to figure out if I'd said what I said.

"I want you to date me."

"What happened with Cassandra?"

"We didn't click."

"It sure looked like you did." She scoffed. "I find it hard to believe Cassandra doesn't click with everyone she meets."

"Well, we didn't and I need someone to go out publicly with. Why not you?"

"Why not me? You heard your mother. It may no longer be a clause in the contract, but it's clear it's still cause for concern." She pursed her lips. I wanted to lean in and kiss them. "Besides, we barely get along."

"We've been getting along just fine."

"You're right." She tilted her head. "Where's the Queen Mother? What does she say about this?"

"She's not back from her stay in the city. She doesn't know about this and doesn't have to. I'm making the decision."

"Oh, you're making the decision." She nodded, pursing her lips. "Good to know."

"If you'll agree." I exhaled. "Why do you make everything so complicated?"

"Why do you assume everyone will agree to your demands?"

"Because they usually do."

"Right. Because they're all puppets. I'm not a puppet."

"I know you're not. That's one of the reasons this will work. Everyone knows you have your own mind and wouldn't be coerced into this."

"Isn't that what you're trying to do though? Coerce me into it?"

"By what, bringing you breakfast and asking you how you're feeling? Last I checked, that was called being nice."

"Which you're not, which means you want something."

"Fine. I want this."

"A fake relationship with me." She shook her head in disbelief. "No one will buy it, least of all your brother."

"Who cares? It's not him we need to convince. It's the public."

"I still don't see the point, or why I'd agree after everything."

"It'll ensure the media attention doesn't fall on Oscar. We wouldn't want him to be caught up in their visceral grip, would we?"

"There it is." She laughed. "The bribe."

"Please, Joslyn?" I set my hand over hers and looked in her eyes so that she wouldn't turn away. "I need to protect my son and his mother, who's still in the hospital, and I'm tired of pretending I have any interest in women on a list."

She nodded ever so slowly and licked her lips. "Fine, but being that I'm agreeing to this and I also happen to practically be your secretary, you need to give me full control of everything we tell the media."

"You always have full control."

"I mean it. No trying to rewrite my stories." She raised an eyebrow.

"I wouldn't dream of it. I trust you implicitly." I squeezed her hand in mine and as I said the words I realized how true they were. I trusted her and in my experience that had more weight than love.

CHAPTER THIRTEEN

JOSLYN

I couldn't believe I agreed to it. I definitely didn't want the media all over Oscar though and considering the fact that they would be opening the palace doors to them in a week, it made sense to take their attention from the boy and put it on a shiny relationship. Aramis stood up to leave and looked around.

"I'm going riding with Oscar. Do you want to join us?"

"Um. Yeah, sure. I guess I might as well get out of here for a bit."

"You don't have to if you don't feel up to it." His brows pulled a bit and I knew he was dying for me to talk about what happened with David.

"I'll join you. Just give me a few minutes to get dressed. I don't think Oscar would approve of me going riding in my pajamas."

"I wouldn't mind." His gaze lowered to the long-sleeve shirt I was wearing and my nipples perked up in an instant. This was exactly why I shouldn't have agreed to dating him, fake or not.

"If you want, I'll meet you in the stables." I stood up and began clearing the table, anything to get away from him quickly.

"I'll wait for you. Rose is taking Oscar and I told her I'd meet them there, so I'm sure she won't mind waiting a few more minutes."

I set everything down in the kitchenette and rushed to my bedroom, shutting and locking the door behind me. Closing the door was just common decency, but the lock was the chaperone between us. I didn't trust either of us in a cottage by ourselves. It was a ridiculous thought being that I'd spent the last six months barging into his apartment, into his bedroom, stopping parties, but the air between us felt different now. It had been the entire time we'd been here. I tried not to think about it. I shouldn't think about it, especially now that I'd agreed to pretend we were dating. Instead of waiting to tell the family with him, I pulled out my phone to send a text message to Adeline. She was the Queen, after all. The Queen and one of my best friends. My other best friend was Pilar, the Princess. My mother often joked that some royalty had to rub off on me because of who my friends were. Adeline wasn't born into it though; she'd married into it, and despite my reservations about her jumping headfirst into a family like theirs, she was happy and thriving. I set my phone down without texting. How could I explain this in a simple text? It would be impossible. Besides, I hadn't even told her David and I were no longer. I'd have to wait.

I finished dressing in warm clothes in case the temperatures dropped during our ride and walked outside to find Aramis lounging on the couch, ankle over his knee and arms extended like he was watching a football game. I stepped into view and realized he was, then frowned.

"Since when do you watch American football?"

"Adeline put me on to it." He shrugged a shoulder. "It's not bad."

"Adeline is entirely too American." I shook my head. She wasn't, not really, her father was French and her mother was Spanish, but somehow her years in American boarding school completely nixed it.

"America has a lot of pros." He turned off the television and stood, tossing the remote.

"Maybe we should look for a woman for you in America then." I raised an eyebrow. Aramis chuckled, that deep laughter that made my throat catch and my heart seize.

"I don't think we need to start jumping continents to find someone, Joslyn."

"We might as well. There don't seem to be enough

women here for you. At least not suitable ones to your standards."

"I don't believe I ever said that." He squinted and fought a smile as he twirled a gray scarf around his neck.

"You didn't have to outright say it." I started walking to the door, while he trailed behind me, shutting the door behind us. "By the way, how did I end up in your bed last night?"

"I carried you there." He said it so matter-of-fact, I stopped dead in my tracts and stared up at him. He still looked entirely too amused by all of this.

"I know that, but why?"

"Because you fell asleep on the couch."

"You could have woken me up and let me go to my cottage or the third bedroom."

"I could have." He shrugged a shoulder, pausing at the side door that led to the stables.

"So why didn't you?"

"You ask too many questions." Aramis shook his head, opening and letting go of the door as we walked into the area. "Too many of the wrong questions."

"What are the right questions?" I frowned, pausing momentarily as he walked ahead. The sound of the latch clicking behind me set me into motion again and I sped up. "What are the right questions?"

He sighed heavily, turning back to me. "Why wouldn't I?"

"What?"

"It's not a matter of why I didn't wake you up, it's a matter of why wouldn't I want you in my bed?"

My heart thumped louder as his words sank in. His expression turned mischievous, the way it often did, the kind my head and heart constantly battled against. He took one step closer to me, too close. The wind picked up and whirled around us. He brought a hand up and brushed a strand of hair back into my high ponytail, and chuckled when the strand fell right back down. His proximity, the scent of his familiar cologne, and the way his gaze seemed to burn into mine were making it nearly impossible for me to breathe. When I finally did catch my breath, it was to denounce this, whatever this was.

"We can't do this," I breathed.

"Do what?"

"This pretend-dating thing you want to do. This . . . whatever this is."

"Why not?" He didn't even bother to wipe away his amusement. All it did was tick me off.

"Because we can't." I stepped away and waved a hand toward him. "You're being too nice to me. No one is going to buy into that."

"I can't be nice?" he laughed.

"Not to someone you don't want to fuck, no."

"Well, then, I can't disagree there." He shrugged a shoulder.

My mouth fell open. Was he saying . . . was he . . . did he want to . . . with me? Me? I blinked, shaking my head.

Surely not. "I'm not going to be a notch on your bedpost. Again. I refuse to be one."

"That's fair."

"So then . . . " I shook my head again. "I don't understand you."

"I don't understand you either, so we're even."

"I want to just be friends. Be cordial. Be able to work with you and do my job well. That's it."

"Your job is literally to find me a suitor and you already agreed to pretend to be my suitor, so I think you've done quite a good job."

"Pretending to be your girlfriend is not part of my job description."

"It is now." He looked me straight in the eye.

"I'm beginning to think we shouldn't do this."

"You want to keep your job, right?"

"Well, yeah, obviously."

"So you'll pretend to be my girlfriend. Otherwise, I have no use for you and you won't need this job title."

"Are you threatening to fire me?" My mouth fell open. "Must I remind you that it's not you I answer to, but the King and Pilar as well?"

"Must I remind you that the King is my brother and will side with me on anything?"

"Must I remind you that the Queen is my best friend and has the King wrapped around her pinky?" I raised an eyebrow, trying to keep my cool, all the while my blood was boiling and he was as cool as a cucumber. I wanted to punch him. I clenched my fists and held them tightly at my sides so I wouldn't succumb to that.

"Look, it's simple. You need a job. I need a girlfriend. We're friends. You know me better than anyone. Besides, you already agreed to this."

"Friends?" I shouted. "You think we're friends? Did you . . . do you hear yourself when you speak to me?"

He cocked his head and nodded a few times. "I need to work on that."

"I'm glad you realize it."

"I do, now, will you be my girlfriend, Joslyn?"

"What are you, thirteen?" I rolled my eyes.

"Is that a yes? I'm taking it as a yes."

"I already said I'd do it. I don't know why we're having this conversation."

"Oscar will start calling out for us any minute and I need to make sure we're on the same page."

"Don't you think we should tell him it's pretend?" I chewed my bottom lip. "I don't like lying to kids."

"Kids have big mouths. If we tell him it's pretend, everyone will know and then what's the point of the ruse at all?"

"You want to lie to them? To the King, the Queen, your family—about this?" I raised an eyebrow. "You know what happens to people who lie to The Crown."

"Baby, I am The Crown. Let me worry about the consequences." He winked before walking away, and damn if I didn't feel it between my legs.

CHAPTER FOURTEEN

"Y OU'RE MY DAD'S GIRLFRIEND?" OSCAR ASKED, frowning.

"It appears so." I smiled, but it was shaky. I didn't want to lie to the boy, but Aramis was right, kids didn't know how to shut up.

"Does that mean he's not going to marry my maman?"

"I don't know," I whispered, my chest squeezing at the thought.

It hadn't even occurred to me that Oscar was holding out hope for his parents to be together. It made sense. I was only eight years old when my own parents divorced, and held out hope that they'd change their mind and stay together. It never happened, of course, and later on I understood why they weren't meant to be together, but still, that hope was always there, hiding somewhere in my heart. Suddenly, I felt bad about all of this. I felt bad about lying to Oscar, like I knew I would. I felt bad that I'd lie to my best friends, though I still wasn't sure what would happen when I told them. I couldn't imagine them believing me. What was worse was that I didn't like the idea of Aramis being with Oscar's mother. I hadn't met Esmée, but judging her based on her son, I was sure she was kind. Why didn't I like the idea of her being with Aramis then? We were just friends, after all. Friends who had hooked up in the past. Way back in the day. And yet . . . I shook the thought away quickly.

"Are you ready to go for a ride?" I smiled at Oscar.

"I think so. I've never ridden before."

"No?"

His curls bounced as he shook his head. I smiled genuinely. He was too cute not to smile at.

"Well, I think you'll love it."

"Dad says I have to ride with Monsieur Paul."

"Oh? Why doesn't your dad let you ride with him?"

"He says you are." Oscar leaned in closer. "He says you're scared to ride alone and Monsieur Paul is a professional so he's going to teach me better."

"I am not scared to ride alone." I scoff-laughed.

"No?" Oscar's brows lifted and I instantly felt bad for lying about something else.

"Only a little scared," I admitted. "I had a bad fall when I was about your age. It landed me in the hospital."

"Do you think I'll fall?"

"Not with Monsieur Paul around. He really is a professional. I heard he used to race horses when he was young."

"Really?" Oscar gasped.

"Really."

"Cool." He grinned as he stood up and started running around me on the grass.

We'd been told to stand off to the side while Rose helped her father by feeding the animals and he finished preparing the horses for the ride. Rose's family was the perfect example of people who had been working for The Crown their entire lives and would stand by their sides no matter what. It seemed like a lot of their employees were like that. Except for their secretaries. The Crown had a long list of secretaries, one for each member of the family, who had quit. King Elias decided to make it so that he and Adeline shared one secretary, John, an older man who was more like a second father and confidant. And then there was me, who was here to serve both Princess Pilar and Prince Aramis. At their beck and call. The job had been interesting, to say the least, especially when the Queen Mother had been the one appointing me places. Now that it was solely up to Aramis and Pilar, it had been . . . better? Worse? I wasn't sure, but judging on my newest task, I knew things wouldn't end well for me. I already envisioned myself packing a bag like all the previous secretaries.

"Are you ready?" My head snapped up to see Aramis standing over me. I looked around and realized Oscar was being helped on a horse. "Sure. Yes. I must have zoned out."

"You looked very pensive. You didn't even notice my arrival." He offered me his hand and I took it to stand, brushing away any loose grass that may be on my pants. "What were you thinking about?"

"All of the secretaries that met their demise before my arrival."

"Their demise?" Aramis chuckled deeply. "How so?"

"Well, they all quit, or were driven out of here, I guess."

"And you think you'll quit?"

"Maybe. I guess it depends how all of this plays out."

"This ride?" He perked an eyebrow, shooting me a sideways glance as we walked toward the horses. He was entirely too good-looking for his own good. For my own good.

"This pretend relationship."

"Ah, that." He glanced away to hide a smile.

"I hate that you're so amused by all of it."

"Am I? I wasn't aware."

"You're clearly amused. You keep smiling and laughing every time I bring it up."

"Because your reaction is funny. You seem to think anyone will care that we're together."

"We're not together. I think everyone will care that we're lying to them once they find out it's all for show."

"Don't worry about that." He shrugged a shoulder.

"Look at me, Pa!" Oscar shouted, grinning from ear to ear.

"You look great up there, Mon Grand." Aramis grinned back.

"We'll take the short route," Monsieur Paul said. "Rose will ride Sally alongside us."

Sally was a beautiful white horse that looked a lot like the one Monsieur Paul and Oscar were riding.

"I'll take Mademoiselle Joslyn with me," Aramis said. "We'll catch up by the rose garden."

Monsieur Paul tapped the horse lightly with his feet and rode off, Rose closely beside them, talking to Oscar.

"Why didn't you ride with Oscar?" I followed Aramis into the stable, where his horse was waiting. I knew it was his because I'd seen him riding once when I visited with Pilar here. Shadow was the name of the horse, and he was a striking black stallion.

"I thought it would be best if Monsieur Paul began teaching him the basics."

It was a fair point, of course, being that Paul knew more about horses than all of us combined, but still. I shook my head. "You know the basics. I know the basics."

"Did you want to ride with my son?" Aramis raised an eyebrow as he took hold of Shadow's reins and began putting them on him slowly, petting and kissing the animal as if it too were his son and dammit if that didn't make my heart flip. I glanced away. I needed to get a hold of my emotions if I was going to survive this.

"No, I'm fine riding with you."

He smirked, his green eyes aglow with a new sort of defiance, and I knew I was in trouble.

CHAPTER FIFTEEN

ARAMIS

I LIKED THE WAY HER ARMS FELT WHEN THEY WERE WRAPPED around me. I liked the way her legs squeezed my hips as we rode the stallion. Unfortunately, my cock liked it too much. I needed to get a grip. I was a man, not a schoolboy. It was the closest Joslyn and I had been in years though. Sure, she showed up at my parties to break them up and tell people to go home. Sure, she helped me pack my bags for trips and went over my schedules every day when I was making appearances on behalf of my brother and The Crown. She thought I was this playboy, just like everyone else did, but she didn't realize that I hadn't slept with anyone in over six months now. Gone were my playboy days, not because I wasn't interested in women, but because the last time I tried to get naked in front of one I couldn't do it. I couldn't bare myself to anyone these days, not with the burns I had from the fire. I hadn't even taken my shirt off in front of Joslyn, something I used to do constantly just to watch her blush.

Insecurity was something I'd never dealt with in life, not before this, and I hated it. I used to preach about how everyone should be accepting of their bodies, their flaws. I'd always been an admirer of all shapes and sizes and used to get upset at women who didn't feel comfortable with their own nudity in front of me. And now I'd become one of them. Joslyn didn't know that though. She had no idea what I was dealing with internally. She had no idea that even though I absolutely relished the way her arms squeezed me as we rode, I was also in pain. She knew I'd been burned in the accident, but had never seen me once they took off my wrappings. The surgeons did an incredible job with skin grafting, but incredible wasn't perfect, and I was used to perfect. When we reached the woods that surrounded the lake, just beyond the rose garden, I asked Shadow to slow down and came to a stop.

"Why are we stopping?" Joslyn's grip loosened around me.

"It's such a beautiful day. Don't you want to enjoy the moment?" I glanced at her over my shoulder. She looked hesitant.

"I guess."

"I want to call the main house and ask them to bring food to the rose garden for us."

"Oh. Okay." She blinked, shaking her head. "I should have thought of that."

"You've been out of sorts today. It's not a big deal."

"Out of sorts?" She frowned as she climbed off the stallion with ease. "I guess I have been."

"It happens to all of us." I hopped down and walked Shadow over to one of the water trenches, tying him loosely to it and filling it with the water from the saddlebag. He immediately started lapping at it.

"Tomorrow I'll have my head on straight," she said and I knew she wasn't joking; her voice was as serious as her expression when I turned to face her.

"You can take a few days if you want."

"No. I don't need a few days. I'm fine."

"Are you sure?" I felt my brow raise. "What's David going to think when we announce that we're dating?"

"You ask me that now? After you sold me on the idea and then basically blackmailed me for good measure?" She laughed.

"In all honestly, I couldn't care less what David thinks about it or how he feels." I shrugged a shoulder. "I'm asking because I want to know how you feel about him knowing."

"I don't feel anything. We broke up. It won't matter to him."

"Ah, yes, you broke up. I had a feeling that was why

you agreed to this." I glanced away from her, at the small lake a few steps away from us. The lake I'd swum more times than I could count. The lake I had skinny-dipped in, had sex in. All things we couldn't do right now even if we wanted to. It wasn't freezing today, but it was still too cold to step foot in it.

"I agreed because it's not the dumbest idea you've ever come up with."

"I'm flattered you think so." I couldn't help my laugh. Joss had a way of backwards complimenting me that I loved.

"I just don't think we should lie to everyone about it," she said a little quieter. "Oscar doesn't like it."

"He said that? I thought he'd be thrilled."

"He thinks you should get together with his mother. Can you blame the boy?" Joslyn's lip turned into a small smile. A sad smile.

I looked at the lake again. I'd been with my fair share of women in my day. Married, engaged, with short- and long-term boyfriends. The way I saw it, their relationship status wasn't my problem. If they wanted to spend a night with me, who was I to refuse? Of course, that was how Oscar had come into all of this. One drunken night with Esmée and boom, a consequence. The good kind of consequence, if you asked me, though I'm sure at the time I would not have seen it that way. I looked at Joslyn again.

"I wouldn't want to hurt Esmée. Hurting her would

mean hurting Oscar. I would never put her in that situation."

"So instead you'll hurt me since I'm expendable to you."

"I never said you were." I stepped forward, closing the distance between us. Joss took a step back, crashing into the trunk of the tree behind her.

"You treat me like I am."

"When, Joslyn? When have I ever treated you like you're expendable to me?" I stepped closer still, my breath tickling her face.

I wasn't even touching her, but I knew she was finding it difficult to speak right now. I wasn't even sure how I was still speaking. All of my blood seemed to travel south of my waist.

"You've never treated me like I wasn't. To you, I'm just another girl. Another notch on your bedpost, aren't I?"

"Never." I shook my head, the tip of my nose flicking hers. "I've never seen you as that."

"You've acted like it, with your flirting, with your parties, with your—"

I reached out, grabbed the back of her neck, and kissed her before she had a chance to finish her sentence. She moaned into my mouth, as I moaned into hers, deepening the kiss as the swell of my heart, of my cock, threatened to make me combust. She tore away, her gaze wild on mine.

"Why did you kiss me?"

"How could I not?"

"Because . . . you don't even like me. This is all pretend. We should draw the line somewhere—"

I kissed her again, breaking the kiss only to drag my lips down her neck, tickling just over the swells of her breasts. I wanted nothing more than to tear the shirt she had on down and suck her nipples into my mouth, but I didn't want to push her, not yet, not until I knew for certain she wanted this just as much as I did. When her hands gripped the collar of my shirt, pleading, begging, I knew she did, but I also knew that it would mean exposing myself, baring myself to her, in a way I wasn't sure I was able to do just yet. It would mean giving her my full trust, and that was where I drew the line. At least for now. I stepped away and walked over to Shadow instead, taking as many deep breaths as I could to shake off the desire.

CHAPTER SIXTEEN

JOSLYN

Holy shit. He kissed me. He kissed me and I felt it down to my very core. It was unlike what I'd experienced with David. It was unlike what I'd experienced any time recently with any man. I thought butterflies and excitement was something I wouldn't experience again until Aramis's lips touched mine and showed me otherwise. He pulled away so suddenly that I had to remind myself to breathe again without his mouth on mine. We didn't speak the remainder of the ride to the indoor rose garden. He didn't even look at me as we got off the horse and walked over to where Oscar, Rose, and Monsieur Paul were. I hated the way my chest caved knowing that he regretted

something that made me come alive. I watched as Oscar ran up to his father and bonded over horse riding, something that I definitely didn't want to discuss. Obviously, I had no qualms about getting on one. I just didn't want to talk about competing on one. Instead of pretending to listen to their conversation, I walked around the garden and busied myself that way.

"Isn't it amazing?"

"It smells lovely in here." I smiled, turning to look at Rose. "It's a nice flower to be named after."

"I've always thought so." She smiled wide, a blush on her cheeks. She met my eyes. "Are you feeling better?"

"I . . ." I felt myself frown. "I guess I am. Thank you."

"I helped Miss Cassandra with her bag as she was leaving this morning."

"It was presumptuous of her to bring a bag."

"I thought so as well." Rose let out a soft laugh. "I guess she assumed she'd charm Prince Aramis."

"I bet she's used to charming everyone."

"I'm sure you are as well."

"Me?" I laughed. "I wouldn't say that."

"You're charming," Rose argued. "And pretty. And kind. Kinder than Miss Cassandra."

"Was she not nice this morning?"

"She was short. Not mean, not nice. Mother always says the true mark of a person is how they act when nobody is looking."

"Your mother is right."

"I bet you've met a lot of people."

"I have and very few have been genuinely charming."

"Do you think the Prince is genuinely charming?"

I glanced away quickly to hide my blush, but felt myself nod in agreement and when I looked at her again, I smiled. "I think the entire royal family is genuinely charming."

"That's what Mother says as well." Rose smiled.

That wasn't entirely true. The Queen Mother was calculatedly charming. Her late husband, from what I remember, was the same. Some people use their charm as a weapon, to hypnotize and maintain control of people. Others can't help their charm. Unlike their parents, Elias, Aramis, and Pilar were charming without trying to be. Maybe it was something they were taught from the time they were kids. Who knew with these families. Maybe it was something they were born with somehow, though one could argue that anything born from such controversy couldn't be as good as they were. If I didn't know them, I'd probably feel that way about them, but I knew them well and they were legitimately good people. It was a good thing too, now that the throne and future of The Crown was in their hands.

"Are you ready?" Aramis called out. Rose and I turned our heads in his direction and walked over. "I'm taking Oscar back. You can ride with Rose."

I couldn't find my voice to speak, so I merely nodded and followed Rose to the horse she'd ridden on. It wasn't that I minded being bossed around by my boss; it was that even though he was my boss, I knew him as an ex-lover, a friend, a foe, and now a fake boyfriend. All of those things combined made for tricky emotions. I already knew that, but now, as I was dismounting the horse that carried me back to the stables, it was cemented. I had feelings for Aramis and I was playing with fire.

"Define dating." Pilar's eyes narrowed on me.

"Yes, please, define dating," Adeline added beside her.

We were having tea in the library, surrounded by stockings Adeline wanted help putting on the fireplace mantle. Pilar thought it was cute. I'd decided she'd watched entirely too many Christmas movies. They were both giving me their full, undivided attention as they sipped their tea, which was comical considering I'd tried to sit down and talk to them about things we actually needed to be doing, like planning a wedding for the Princess and making sure everything was ready for the King and Queen's first child, and they'd been avoiding all of those responsibilities.

"We thought we'd try it out." I shrugged, lifting my own cup. "We spent time together last night and—"

"Was that the reason David was so upset?" Pilar asked.

I focused on my tea. I'd prepared for this question, knowing it would come, but still felt rather awful lying about it. Finally, I set the cup down and nodded.

"We had a misunderstanding about Aramis. I didn't cheat on David, not that he and I were official or anything, but still. It was . . . a misunderstanding."

"Hm." Pilar stared at me as Adeline blinked, as if she was confused by all of this.

"But you hate Aramis," she said finally. I lifted the glass to my lips again.

"I don't hate him. I just . . . well, in any event, you know what they say about love and hate. I mean, look at you and Elias."

"True." Adeline frowned slightly. "I guess it does make sense."

"I always had a feeling you were secretly in love with my brother."

"Love?" I sputtered, choking on my tea. "I never said I was in love with him. I said we're going to try this out. The dating thing."

"Love is a possibility though." Adeline smiled wide.

"And then we'd all be sisters," Pilar added with a mischievous smile of her own.

"No. I'm . . . please don't start." I shot them a pointed look. "We're supposed to be planning Pilar's wedding and setting everything up for the baby and neither of you have paid any attention to that so don't even think about a wedding between Aramis and me."

"I think I want to elope," Pilar said, a whispered admission.

"What?" Adeline and I both shouted.

"You can't elope; your mother will kill us all," Adeline said.

"My mother isn't even here for holiday anymore. She fucked things up with my brothers, and with me as a matter of fact, and well, I'm an adult and I'll do what I want."

"Okay well then I'm speaking up against it," Adeline said. "You'll regret not having a wedding. My God, can you imagine what the newspapers will say about their very own princess not sharing her big day with them?"

"Who cares about them? They've never treated us fairly before."

"They've watched you grow up," I said softly. "They'll want to continue watching you grow up. Besides, it's not like you can escape them."

"My entire life has been a media circus. I want this to be mine. Intimate."

"So we'll make it intimate. Family and friends only."

"Ben has a million family members."

"And you think Ben's mother is going to just let him run off and elope?" I raised an eyebrow.

"I guess not." Pilar scowled. "Maybe we can just do it here. They'll be here for Christmas anyway."

"In a week," I said. "That's a week from now."

"Less than a week." Adeline looked worried. "It's like five days from now."

"Do you think we can pull it off?" Pilar bit her lip.

"I know we can. Do you want media invited or not?"

Pilar looked at Adeline, who without saying a word made her stance clear: yes to the media. Pilar sighed heavily and glanced at me.

"I'll make sure only the really nice ones are invited," I said. "Maybe we should consider selling the photos to a magazine?" I looked at Adeline.

"I'm not sure Elias would be okay with that considering he's still trying to win over the public after his father's awful reign." She cringed. "No offense, P."

"None taken." Pilar shrugged. "So, five days. Oh my God. I need to go tell the groom." She stood up as we all laughed. Ben was going to flip out.

"Well, I guess we better get to work," Adeline said, standing. "I have to go tell Eli about this. You can keep telling me about this new . . . boyfriend of yours later."

"Wait."

She turned around, hand on the door.

"Should I write something for the media . . . about Aramis and me?"

"I don't see why you have to." She shrugged a shoulder. "They'll be too focused on the wedding to care."

As she walked out of the room, I realized that it was something I should be happy about, but wasn't.

CHAPTER SEVENTEEN

T HAD BEEN THREE DAYS SINCE I'D SPOKEN TO ARAMIS. I'D SEEN him, of course. He popped his head into every room Adeline, Pilar, and I were working in to make a sly remark about us running out of time. Typical Aramis shit. I was busy. Busy with flowers and catering. Busy with security and narrowing down magazines and journalists. Busy trying to convince the Queen Mother that she needed to return to Versailles in time for the wedding, and that was where my patience was running thin. I was used to the royal family. Used to their inconveniences and demands and even their occasional meltdowns when they didn't get their way. I thought myself lucky, since I knew how to navigate all of that, how to ensure everyday life would run smoothly for them. The Queen Mother I did not know how to handle. There was no manual on how to deal with a sixty-six-year-old spoiled brat who was so used to getting her way that she didn't stop to consider there were other ways. She was upset she didn't get to pick the color of Pilar's bridesmaids' dresses (Pilar chose light pink, the Queen Mother wanted red). She was annoyed about the flowers ("there won't be any poppies in the photographs"). She was even upset that Pilar did not want to hire a famous singer, the way Elias and Adeline had at their wedding, and threatened she'd call someone and hire them behind our backs. It was as though I'd silently been moved from Aramis's secretary to the Queen Mother's handler and if that was the case, I definitely needed a raise. Dealing with imbeciles was beneath my paygrade.

As I took my slippers off and climbed into bed that night, the only thing I had energy for was the heavy sigh that escaped my lips, and as I closed my eyes and tried to rid myself of thoughts of what I needed to do tomorrow, my mind voluntarily floated to Aramis. Was the fake relationship off? I assumed so. If we were supposedly dating, he would have made a show of it in front of his sister-in-law and sister. I knew he was busy with Oscar, making sure he took him to see his mother every day and spending as much time with the boy as he could. Now that Esmée was at home and had all the help in the world since Elias and Aramis sent her a staff of her own, I was sure Oscar would want to go back to his regular life with his mother and the rest of his family. I had no idea what that would look like for him or for Aramis.

My eyes were drifting shut when my phone vibrated and made me jump to pick it up. It was Aramis. I answered it quickly.

"You were sleeping," he said, his voice was warm and deep in my ear.

"Not sleeping. Not yet."

"I feel like I haven't seen you in days."

"That's because you've been avoiding me."

"Avoiding you? You're the one planning a shotgun wedding. Pilar says she's not pregnant, so I don't understand what the rush is."

"Does it matter? It got you off the hook."

"You really don't believe that." He scoffed. "If anything, my younger sister getting married will mean I'll get double the questions. Double the pressure."

"I hadn't thought of that."

"You're an only child."

"You say it like it's a compliment."

"Isn't it?"

"I don't know. Would you want to be an only child?"

"In this family? Absolutely not. That would mean I'd be King."

"Who doesn't want to be King?"

"The only people who want to be King are the ones who don't know what the title entails."

"You're right."

"As usual."

"Funny." I smiled. "What'd you call me for? To tell me how much you miss me?"

"More like to grace you with my voice since I know you missed me."

"Oh, right, of course, which is exactly the reason I called you in the first place."

He chuckled deeply. I smiled wider, biting my lip.

"I've missed this," he said finally after a bout of silence. I was surprised to hear the words and even more surprised to feel the butterflies swarm my belly.

"I have as well."

"I'm surprised you admitted it aloud."

"Me too."

"I still want to date."

"Fake date," I said.

"Sure. Whatever you want to call it."

"Okay." I bit my lip again and finally gathered up the courage to say, "No kissing." And because he stayed quiet and didn't answer right away, I added it one more time, "No kissing when we're alone, or in public for that matter; I'm sure we can go without kissing."

"That's fine."

"Okay, good." I hated the way my heart sank.

I hated that I wanted him to fight me on this one thing and that he didn't seem to care whether he kissed me again or not. If his reaction to it last time was any indication, I shouldn't have been surprised, and yet I was. He wanted me. I felt it. I saw it in his eyes when he looked at me. Maybe I was an idiot for misreading the entire thing.

"You'll be my date to the wedding," he said. "That's kind of assumed since we're dating, but I wanted to state it so there would be no confusion."

"Sure. I mean, we're both in the actual wedding and sitting in the same table at the reception, so I don't think it matters how we get there or leave."

"Like I said, I want no confusion."

"There won't be any."

"Good. Good luck with the rest of the planning. Good night, Joslyn."

"Good night, Aramis."

With that, we hung up. I tossed and turned all night.

CHAPTER EIGHTEEN

"YOU LOOK BEAUTIFUL." I SMILED AT PILAR AS I WALKED into her room.

"Thank you." She turned around and showed me the rest of her gown, which was now completely altered and fit perfectly against her curvy frame. "And thank you again for everything you've done. I knew you could, but it's still . . . I'm in awe."

"And you haven't even seen the reception." I winked.

"I can't wait." She squealed. "I can't believe I'm actually getting married."

"You better believe it after all the work we put into this." I raised an eyebrow. She laughed. The women around her, helping her dress, also laughed lightly.

"Do you know if Tamara and Asher are here?" Pilar asked. "We don't know if Ash fits in his little tuxedo."

"I'm sure he—"

As if on cue, the door opened and Asher, Ben's son, ran inside. His mother followed closely behind him, a bashful smile on her face.

"I'm sorry. He just couldn't wait and the guard said it was okay," Tamara said.

"Are you kidding? We were just talking about you." Pilar moved, making the women hemming her dress stop, and crouched to throw her arms around Asher, kissing his forehead gently, before standing and hugging Tamara.

"You look stunning," Tamara said, pulling away. "The most beautiful bride."

"Thank you. Thank you for coming on such short notice. Is Jack here?"

"He's here. He went to take Ben some cigars he brought him."

"Oh, he'll love those. I just hope he doesn't smoke them before the wedding," Pilar said.

"I'll kill him if he does." Tamara scowled. "I told Jack to wait but he kept going on and on about a humidor, so . . ." She shook her head. "Ben's parents are also here. You owe me for that one."

"Oh my God. They flew in with you?" Pilar laughed.

"Only because I love you." Tamara shook her head.

Pilar laughed louder, then stopped, turning to the small garment bag on the chair beside her. "These are

Asher's tuxedos. We can hem either one if they're too long. I think the photographer wants him to get dressed with Ben for photos."

"I'll take him right over." Tamara grabbed the garment bags and tapped Asher's head. "Let's go get changed for the wedding."

"I'm going to have the most important job," Asher announced to the room. "I'll have the wedding rings and without wedding rings you can't get married."

"Very true." Pilar smiled. "I hope you'll take good care of them for us."

"I'll guard them with my life."

"That's a bit excessive, but thank you." Pilar laughed. I couldn't help but laugh as well.

"He watched a movie about knights on the way over." Tamara shook her head with a chuckle. "Come along, Asher."

"See you in a bit, Ash."

"See you, Princess," he called out, blowing her a kiss as they walked out of the room.

"He's so sweet," one of the seamstresses said.

"Adorable," another added.

"He is." Pilar grinned widely.

Of all the things in the world that could surprise me, the biggest one was my friend's ability to not only accept the fact that her fiancé had a son, but cherish it. She'd stepped into Ben's life seamlessly, as if she'd always been there. Even her relationship with Ben's ex-fiancée was incredible. It was commendable, for sure, but not something I could say I would do if I was in her shoes. It wasn't something I thought she could do either, though, and here she was, showing me differently. The fact that Tamara was kind helped, but it was more than that. I thought of Aramis and Oscar and how much I enjoyed both seeing him as a father and spending time with his little boy, but it wasn't the same. I wasn't actually Aramis's girlfriend and Oscar's mother wasn't Aramis's ex, and still whenever I thought about the possibility of him getting together with Esmée I felt like someone was punching me in the stomach. That was yet another thing I needed to seriously stop.

"I guess we're not walking together." The comment came from David, making my heart sink a little.

"I guess we aren't."

Originally, we were going to walk the wedding together, but last minute, Pilar switched it so that I was walking with Aramis and David was walking with Corina, a friend of hers from primary school. David sighed heavily, adjusting his bowtie. I hated to admit it, but he looked really great in a tuxedo. Then again, David looked good in everything. He was careful about what he ate and watched his figure. He got haircuts every two weeks, like clockwork. He never had stubble on his face, always clean-shaven and handsome. Him looking great in a tuxedo wasn't a surprise.

"I didn't bring a date," he said.

That was a surprise. "Oh."

"I wasn't sure where we stood. You haven't been answering my calls."

"I've been busy planning a wedding."

"You did a good job."

"A good job," I said. Not great, not wonderful, just good. "You could have done better?"

"I hire outside resources to do things that aren't in my job description."

"Meaning you think someone else could have done better." I scoffed, shaking my head. "You do realize I was a wedding planner before I took the job as Pilar's secretary."

"I thought you were Aramis's secretary." David raised an eyebrow.

"I'm . . . no, I'm Pilar's secretary. I was just helping out Aramis."

"I'm sure you were doing more than helping out."

My face burst into flames. I glanced away, jaw ticking, feeling as if he'd slapped me. I couldn't even deny it outright, not if I wanted to keep the charade that Aramis and I started AFTER the fact.

"I've been looking for you." The voice was Aramis's and made me blush even deeper. I shut my eyes. God. What timing. Even when he set his hand on my arm, I didn't dare face them. "We need to go line up."

"I'll be right there."

"Oh. David," he said, all nonchalant. "I wasn't sure you'd make it on such short notice."

"I always make time for those important to me."

At that, I scoffed. The reason David and I had never gotten serious, at least as far as I knew, was because he rarely made time to see me. He was all work, work, work, like Rhianna, but less pretty and definitely less badass. I met his eyes then, his expression cold and hard, and matched it with my own. I was tired of playing the wounded bird around men like David. I'd been doing it my entire life and it really didn't suit the woman I'd become.

"It was nice seeing you, David." I nodded politely and began walking away, but Aramis held my wrist, forcing me to stop walking. I didn't turn around again.

"We'll see you around," Aramis said before sliding his hand down to mine and leading me away from David.

I could only imagine the infuriating look on his handsome face. It was probably very much like my own. I waited until we were in the hall before yanking my hand from Aramis's and glaring at him.

"What the hell was that about?"

"What was what about?"

"That scene you just caused. What was that about?"

"I didn't cause a scene. I was merely fetching you because we need to go get ready to walk my sister's wedding."

"I think I know when we're supposed to be ready to go." My eyes narrowed on his entirely too amused green eyes. "We still have ten minutes before we have to gather in the Galerie des Glaces."

"It's beyond me why my sister would want to get married surrounded by haunted mirrors."

"It's beyond me why you have to make a smart remark about everything."

"It's beyond me why you're getting so worked up about nothing. We agreed to date, didn't we? What does it matter if your now ex-boyfriend sees us holding hands?"

"It doesn't . . . this isn't . . . oh my God you're maddening. We agreed to date and then you kissed me and then pretended like it was the worst thing to ever happen in the world and then you ignored me for days upon days until you called me to remind me that our agreement was still on and now you show up in the middle of my conversation with David in which he was trying to make me feel guilty for sleeping in your cottage and talking like the only reason I have a job here to begin with is because you want to get in my pants, but that's all wrong because you obviously don't, despite your little flirtatious bouts." I took a deep breath and let it out once I was finished speaking. Aramis raised one perfect eyebrow.

"Who said I didn't want to get in your pants?"

"Did you not hear anything I just said? It's obvious you don't. You kissed me and then acted like—"

Without warning or preamble, he stepped forward, grabbed my cheeks, and kissed me, his lips hard on mine, his tongue not asking for permission as it found mine. A

moan ripped from my throat, caught by his mouth pressed so closely to mine we were sharing the same oxygen. I felt as though I was floating, because unlike the kiss we shared the other day, this one was raw, unfiltered, and as he pressed his hard body against mine and let me feel his lust for me, I felt myself quickly begin to unravel. The flicker of a camera nearby was what made my feet hit the ground again. I pulled away from Aramis, seeking the culprit and found the photographers I'd invited standing nearby, clicking away and whispering softly to each other.

"I guess the cat's out of the bag," Aramis said, rather loudly.

"Is this a new development?" one of the journalists asked.

"How long have you been together?" another asked.

"I'll answer your questions after my sister's wedding." Aramis winked, grabbed my hand, and walked me into the room we were now supposed to be standing in.

I was still reeling from everything—the fight, the kiss, the photos, his statement to the media—that I didn't have time to focus on any one thing before we had to line everyone up and start walking. My heart was still pounding hard against my chest as we walked. I couldn't even focus on the music, the small guest list sitting on either side of us, or the violinist playing in the corner. I couldn't see the flowers or the other bridesmaids. The only thing I could focus on was taking one step at a time and holding on to Aramis's arm so I wouldn't falter. Had he planned to kiss me in front of those photographers? Had it been staged that way? I wouldn't put it past him. Everyone in this family only looked out for themselves and The Crown and there seemed to be very little they wouldn't do in order to salvage both. I'd told him I would make a statement myself. I told him I'd handle it. As I watched King Elias walk my best friend down the aisle, I pushed aside my irate thoughts and focused on her. She looked stunning. Of course, I'd seen her earlier, but seeing her in this light, with this opulence surrounding us, was unreal.

I couldn't imagine what the ghosts in the room, scandalous as they were rumored to be, must have thought about her very unrevealing gown. We stood there, as the priest held mass and the beautiful couple proclaimed their loyalty and said their vows, which were generic but somehow made me cry nonetheless. From the other side of the makeshift altar, I caught Aramis looking at me and forced myself to look away. I wasn't one of those people who didn't like showing emotion or crying in front of people. On the contrary, I embraced anything I was feeling and was okay putting it on display, but that wasn't Aramis's way. It wasn't Pilar's or Elias's. These were people who were skilled in not showing their emotions at all. How many times had I warned Adeline against marrying Elias for that very reason? I thought once more about the kiss we'd shared and the photographs that had been taken. Something about it all was unsettling. The way he pulled me out of my conversation with David to do that. The way the journalists knew exactly where we'd be standing, even though they were supposed to be on the other side of the hall. I knew he'd done it on purpose because there was nothing Aramis didn't do on purpose. I just didn't understand why. Everyone cheered and pulled me out of my thoughts once again. I realized Ben and Pilar were sharing their first kiss as newlyweds and smiled, cheering along. They walked down the aisle. King Elias and Queen Adeline followed. Aramis held out his arm for me to take, and I did, ignoring the way my heart launched its way up to my throat once more.

CHAPTER NINETEEN

ARAMIS

I SIPPED MY CHAMPAGNE AND WATCHED JOSLYN AS SHE SPOKE TO David a few feet away from me. I wasn't sure what they were talking about, but it didn't look like a friendly conversation, with the way he kept shaking his head and she kept rolling her eyes. I'd already interrupted them once and didn't want to do it again. Far be it for me to look like a needy boyfriend or childish lover. If Joss wanted to try to mend things with him, she was welcome to try. For starters, we weren't actually dating, and also, it wasn't my place to tell her who she could and couldn't see. That didn't mean I didn't hate the idea of her with him, or any other man, for that matter. Somewhere between the kiss in the woods and tonight, I'd decided that I was ready to commit to something real with her. I just wasn't sure how to tell her. I'd spent the majority of our lives poking her and making her think that I wasn't interested. How does one go from uninterested in a person to full-on committed? Furthermore, how does an assumed commitment-phobe give into commitment? I wasn't sure. I didn't have any of those answers. The only thing I knew for sure was that I was done playing the field and wanted to be with someone and that someone was Joslyn. This wasn't something new. I hadn't been able to kick these emotions for almost a year now. In that year, sure, I'd thrown parties and kicked heiresses out of my apartment and left them banging on my door, but I hadn't actually banged them. My accident was tragic. People died. I survived, but a part of me died that day as well. The part of me that took life for granted. And now that I had Oscar, I definitely knew I needed to change, to grow into a man he could be proud to call his father. Something I'd never been proud to call my own.

As if on cue, I felt a tug on the bottom of my jacket and looked down to see Oscar looking up at me.

"Can Asher and I play in the garden?"

"Not tonight. It's dark and cold out." I patted his head. "Where's Rose?"

"She's sitting with Asher." He pointed toward the table and I saw that both Rose and Asher were writing on the linen.

"They're writing on them?" I started walking in that direction and Oscar grabbed my hand as he followed.

Joss was normally paying attention to every detail at weddings and parties that she put together, but tonight was different. Pilar asked her to hire other people to do that for her so that she could enjoy the wedding. Something she would be doing if she wasn't so busy arguing with David, who should be non-consequential at this point since they'd broken up and now we were together. Nevertheless, I'd get to the bottom of this. I stopped in front of the table and both Rose and Asher looked up.

"You can't write on the linen."

"We're not." Rose laughed lightly, lifting the edge of what looked like linen but was white paper. "Joslyn set this area up for the kids, so they wouldn't want to go outside, but Oscar has other ideas."

"I already told him he can't go outside. It's dark and cold out tonight."

"But Joss turned the pretty lights on," Oscar whined. "She said all of us were going outside for pretty lights."

"Well, maybe that'll be later." I frowned wondering what he was talking about.

"Okay." Oscar sighed heavily.

"Oh, come on, Oscar. She even bought you Legos."

"Legos? Where?" he perked up.

"Ah, you haven't even checked beneath the table." Rose winked.

Both Asher and Oscar hopped up and got on their knees

to look underneath the table. There were a lot of "wow" and "cool" remarks. Too many for me not to look for myself. I crouched down and lifted the linen to find glowing lights underneath to light the way for a working train set, a box of Legos, and a separate box with action figures.

"Whoa," Asher said.

"Joslyn really did think of everything," Rose said in awe.

"It appears she did." I stood and looked at Rose. "They have enough entertainment to last all night. You're free to roam the rest of the palace with them, but stay away from the outdoors until it's time. Make sure you get yourself something to eat."

"I will. Thank you, sir."

I walked away and headed toward Joslyn, who was finally no longer speaking to David, but was now standing by the bar speaking to Adeline. Because I was tired of waiting, I walked up to them and joined their conversation, or rather stood there as they finished up talking about the decorations.

"Didn't she do a great job?" Adeline asked, smiling at me.

"Spectacular. She even thought about the children," I said. "They have enough entertainment for a month."

"Aw, that's sweet. I'm going to check out their little area," Adeline said, winking at Joss and smiling at me. The way she did that made me wonder what else was said that I hadn't been privy to.

"You've been busy," I said once she was gone.

"Not really. I was just chatting it up with guests."

"With David." I hadn't meant to say his name the way I did, with such distaste, but I also didn't care to explain myself.

"Yeah, he's one of the guests." She glanced away, taking a sip of her wine.

"And?"

"And what?"

"And what agreement did you come to with him? Are you going to keep fucking him even though we said we would be together?"

Her mouth dropped momentarily. "You can't be serious."

"Oh, but I am." I felt myself smile.

It was a façade, this smile. One I used to both charm and piss people off. One Joss had been on the receiving end more times than I could count. Her eyes narrowed on mine and she shook her head as she walked away. I ordered a drink and turned to watch as her hips sashayed out of the room. I knew I was going to piss her off and maybe I was wrong for it, but I was upset myself. The thought of her trying to patch things up with David was entirely too maddening for me to come to terms with. So what if what Joss and I were doing wasn't real, I didn't want to have to see her with another man. It would be an embarrassment for me, especially now that the rags got our picture together. It was with that thought in mind that I picked up the glass of champagne the bartender handed me and went off to find Joslyn.

CHAPTER TWENTY

JOSLYN

'D JUST FINISHED SPEAKING TO THE MAN IN CHARGE OF THE fireworks when I turned to see Aramis walking over. It was a chilly night, but we had heaters lined up and set up outside to help with that. I knew the moment he walked past one, because his footsteps slowed and he looked around momentarily.

"You really did think of everything." He tucked a hand into his pocket and held his champagne flute in the other.

"I tried."

"You're upset."

"When did you start caring about my being upset?" I raised an eyebrow.

"I'm not sure." He took a sip of his champagne. "Maybe tonight."

"Did you stage the kiss earlier?"

"You haven't put out a statement."

I shook my head. I knew he'd done it but hearing him clarify it like this was annoying. "The Princess just got married. Did you stop for a second to think that maybe that kiss will make headlines and take away from her big day?" I crossed my arms, uncrossed them, and started walking inside with him on my tail. "No, of course you didn't. You only think about yourself."

"I asked you to do this weeks ago and you didn't."

"It hasn't been weeks. It has been a week." I turned to face him once we were inside the palace. "I'm tired of people trying to take over my job as if I don't know what I'm doing or what's best for everyone."

"If you'd done it when I asked you to, I wouldn't have had to stage that photo."

"If you'd had a little patience, you wouldn't have ruined your sister's wedding."

"I hardly ruined her wedding." He scoffed, setting the empty flute down on the nearest table. "You think one headline is going to ruin her wedding? You're crazy."

"Maybe I am crazy, but not for thinking that. Maybe I'm crazy for thinking I could work with you and agreeing to be in a fake relationship with you."

"Stop calling it a fake relationship. Besides, you were fine with it earlier when your lips were against mine."

"I was distracted."

"You were distracted when you were kissing me? It sure didn't feel that way."

"I don't know why we're having this conversation. I said no more kissing and the first thing you did was kiss me and you did it for the rags, to boot."

"Are you mad because I went behind your back about that or because you don't have a shot at getting back together with David now?" He stepped forward.

I turned around and stepped into the first door that opened. If we were going to have this conversation, it would be someplace I knew the photographers wouldn't be. Unfortunately, the room I stepped into was dark and unknown to me. Aramis stepped in and shut the door behind him. I turned around to face him and realized that even though I couldn't see him, he was much too close to me. I shook my head and focused on the conversation.

"Why are you so obsessed with David?"

"I'm not."

"You obviously are. You've brought him up twice in one night. I didn't realize you were this insecure."

"I'm not." I could hear the frown in his voice and took his momentary confusion to pose a different question.

"Why did you act the way you did when you kissed me in the woods?"

"How did I act?"

"You kissed me and then pretended I didn't even exist."

"I was riding with my son."

"You used him as a shield and you know it."

"This is ridiculous. I can't have a conversation in the dark." He walked away and switched on a lamp. It was still dark, but it was better now that more than just the moon was illuminating the room.

"You were using him so that you wouldn't have to confront the kiss."

"Confront the kiss?" He closed the distance between us once more. "Have you forgotten we've shared a lot more than a kiss? Or did you just store that away in the furthest end of your memory so that you don't have to think about it?"

"No." I swallowed, heart racing. "I remember quite well."

"Do you?" His voice lowered and he stepped closer still. My stomach flipped once and flipped again when he brought a hand up to my face. "Do you need to be reminded?"

"Are you going to remind me?"

"I can."

"Right now?" I felt out of breath and nothing was even happening.

"Why not?" His lips on mine silenced whatever response I was sure to make.

The kiss was soft, slow, a complete departure from our previous ones, even the few we shared all those years ago. He took his time with his tongue exploring my mouth as his hands slowly made their way down the sides of my

arms, each calloused pad on his hands grazing my soft skin as they lowered down to the skirt of my dress. He pulled it up ever so slowly, as if to give me time to say no. What I did was lean into him, reach my hands up behind his head and tug his thick head of hair to announce my stance—I wanted this, I wanted him. Now. It seemed to fuel him. His kiss turned deeper, more demanding, his tongue whipping mine as he tucked a hand into my panties and slid his fingers into the lips of my already wet pussy, a relentless tease as he explored.

"It's too bad we don't have much time," he said against my lips as he pulled away from the kiss. He took his fingers out of my panties and brought them to his mouth, sucking on them as he looked into my eyes and moaned as if the taste was the best thing in the world. "I'll take my time with you next time."

"Next time?" I gasped as he once again slid his fingers into my panties, this time sliding them inside of me and pumping. "Oh my God."

"You're so wet, Joslyn. Have you been this wet all night?"

"No." I shook my head, gasping and arching my back. "Don't stop doing that."

"Were you this wet for David?"

"No." I gasped once more when his thumb hit my clit.

"No?" He pressed his chest against me, continuing his relentless strokes.

"No dammit. Please don't stop."

"I'm not stopping, baby," he whispered against my mouth. "Later tonight, after the party is over, you're going to come to my cottage and I'm going to fuck you."

"Okay." My eyes were blurring with lust, with need, with the building orgasm.

"And when we're finished, you're going to sleep in my bed."

"Okay."

"Good." He pressed his finger against my clit, rubbing circles as his other fingers moved inside of me, and I felt myself come apart on his hands.

CHAPTER TWENTY-ONE

ARAMIS

Even after I'd washed my hands, I smelled her on my fingers. It did nothing to help with the situation inside my pants. The only thing keeping me at this party was the fact that it was my sister's wedding and I couldn't haul Joslyn out of it to fuck her right now. I was fully regretting not fucking her earlier, but I was trying to think clearly and didn't know how much time she had, being that she was setting up the fireworks and whatever else was happening behind the scenes. I figured that had to give me some kind of points, the fact that I was being respectful of her job, despite going behind her back with the photographers. The rest of the wedding was a blur. My eyes were on Joslyn's ass the entire time. My brother gave the toast. Even as Joslyn made her toast, I couldn't seem to focus on anything past the fullness of her lips. By the time it was time for fireworks, Rose came up to me with Oscar and Asher telling me that she would take them both to what was Ben and Pilar's cottage, which they wouldn't be using tonight, for a sleepover. I readily agreed. Anything to make it easier for me to have Joss all to myself. I couldn't remember the last time I was this consumed by a woman. I knew the whole celibacy played a part in it.

The only thing I knew, when I heard the door of my cottage open and shut was that I wanted her more than I wanted anything else in my life in that moment. I stood from my bed, walking over to greet her, and took her in. She was wearing only a white robe and when I came into view, she began undoing the tie and letting it fall open slowly. Her breasts were high and much suppler than I thought. There was a thin line on her pubic bone that I instantly wanted to lick, and curves I longed to explore. She stepped forward, wordlessly, her eyes on mine. There was a definitiveness in them there hadn't been before, as if she'd decided to let herself give into this because there was no other choice. I wasn't sure there was. As I walked over, I took my own clothes off—pulling my shirt over my head and tossing it, lowering my sweatpants and tossing that along with my boxer briefs. I was hard, all of the blood in my body concentrated on my balls, my cock. I reached and stroked it once, twice, picturing what it would be like when I filled her pussy, how she'd grip me. My heart was uncontrollable. This felt like so much more than just sex and we hadn't even yet touched. When the distance between us was finally no longer, we kissed. I couldn't be sure who started it or who would end it, but as her tongue met mine and our fingers gripped each other's hair, I just knew it felt right, real, unlike anything before it. Her hand closed over mine and then replaced it. I groaned against her lips. I used one hand to feel her breast and the other to find her pussy, my fingers sliding into it easily.

"You're so wet, Joslyn."

She mewled, nodding against me.

"You've been wanting this for a long time. Wanting me." I pulled away slightly. "You're not going to deny it?"

"No."

My heart fluttered. "I've wanted you for as long as I can remember."

"Liar." She gasped when I slid another finger inside of her, pumping into her as I found her clit with my thumb.

"I'm not lying. I've talked myself out of this one too many times."

"Why would you . . . why would you . . . Oh my God, don't stop."

I rubbed faster, pumped faster until she came against my hand, then I lifted her into my arms and took her to my bed, laying her out and opening her legs before burying myself between them, kissing and sucking and licking her while she moaned and rotated her hips, spreading her cum over my mouth, my face. I slid a condom on as she panted on the bed and waited for her to come to completely. When she did, she sat up on her elbows and looked at me through long, thick lashes.

"Condom." She nodded. "I'm glad one of us thought of that."

"I'm always prepared." I winked. She bit her lip as she looked at me. It was only then that I remembered how marred my skin was, how scarred from all the burns.

"You're so perfect," she whispered. "How are you so perfect?"

"I'm not." I glanced away, heart pounding. "I look awful. Horrifying."

She sat up on her knees, so that we were almost eye-level, and grabbed both sides of my face. "You're hot, sexy, completely drop-dead gorgeous."

"Stop."

"I won't."

"You don't have to—" I met her gaze again and she kissed me deeply, and when she broke the kiss, she kissed my cheek and made her way down my jaw, my shoulders, my chest.

I shivered with each kiss, each touch. The burns were something I tried so hard to forget, to not even look at, and having her attention on them felt heavy, but made all of this even more real for me because I was letting her do this. I wanted her to do this and I believed her when she called me all of those things. I waited until she straightened again before grabbing both of her breasts into my mouth. She threw her head back with a loud moan, saying my name as she inched closer. I pulled away and positioned her with her back on the bed again. Normally, I would have taken her from behind, and maybe I would later, but right now in this moment I wanted nothing more than to see her face as I slipped into her. My cock was throbbing as it made its way through her folds and into her slowly. She gasped with each bit I slipped in, her back arching when I completely filled her. Our eyes met briefly, for a moment, and then I started to move, fucking her fast, hard, deeply, letting her feel every single part of me the way I felt her pussy gripping my cock. When we came, it was with each other's names spilling from our mouths and I couldn't imagine a more perfect end to an evening.

"I'm clean," I said, later, when we were lying in bed.

"So am I," she said. "And on the pill."

"Maybe next time . . ."

"Next time?"

"You can't think this is the only time." I glanced over at her. "Do you want it to be the only time?"

"No. I don't know." She bit her lip. "I guess I wasn't really thinking about it."

"I definitely want to do this again." I kissed her and pulled her close. "Stay the night."

She nodded, letting out a shuddering breath, and I shut my eyes, drifting to sleep.

CHAPTER TWENTY-TWO

JOSLYN

H E'D ASKED ME TO STAY AND I DID, BUT STILL LEFT BEFORE sunup. I couldn't bear the thought of things being awkward between us today. We had nothing to blame it on. Neither one of us were drunk. We weren't teenagers. We weren't dumb.

I'd just finished drying my hair when I heard the knock on my door. The sound and the anticipation making my heart launch into my ears. I walked slowly toward it, willing myself to calm down, unable to at the thought of having to face Aramis so soon after I'd left his cottage. When I opened the door, it was one of the maids on the other side, her eyes cast down to the floor as to not disrespect me. I hated that the staff was like this, so cautious and careful not to look us in the eye, but I knew it was the former King and Queen Mother's way. They believed the staff was not worthy of looking into their eyes. Even though the rule didn't extend to my position, I hated it. Elias had done a lot to try to make them feel welcome, but the damage was done, and so, Adeline did everything she could to make them feel comfortable, much to the Queen Mother's distaste.

"The Queen Mother wishes to have breakfast with you," the young woman said.

"With me?" My confusion must have rung through in my voice because she finally looked up at me and nodded.

"She asked for you."

"I'll be right over." I waited until the young girl walked away before closing the door and rushing to finish getting ready.

I hadn't planned on seeing the Queen Mother at all today. I'd managed to avoid her at all costs last night during the wedding. Before then, she'd managed to avoid everyone else, choosing to dress quietly by herself in her wing of the palace and only opting to show up for photographs with Pilar and Ben. Even that had been awkward to see, the heavy silence that seemed to accompany her arrival. It was as though no one wanted to speak around her. No one wanted to invite any negativity around the wedding. I'd personally never had a problem with her. She'd always been very nice to me, cordial. She asked me about my family and how I was doing before getting down to business, and always smiled when she said goodbye. The Queen Mother wasn't known for her small talk or being overly friendly, but she was just. She'd been welcoming with Adeline once she got past the idea that her son, the King, would be marrying a commoner. Before the drama with Aramis and the child she hid from him, she'd been very involved in Adeline's pregnancy. I wondered how involved she was now. I wouldn't be surprised if Adeline continued to keep in touch with her. It wasn't like Addie to write people off, regardless of how big the mistakes they made were. It was something everyone admired about her. I shook myself off as I prepared to open the door and walk to the palace for breakfast with the Queen Mother. I'd never been nervous around her before, but I also wasn't dating her son, her favorite son, the last time I saw her. Now that I was, I couldn't quite shake the nerves.

The entire walk to the palace, I blamed my shiver on the cool breeze that swirled around me, but deep down I knew it was nerves. When I reached the door, the butler opened it and ushered me to the main dining hall, where the Queen Mother was sitting down at the end of the large, fifty-person-seater table.

"Joslyn. Thank you for joining me." Her lips turned up slightly upon seeing me.

"Of course." I gave a slight curtsy in front of her chair before sitting down in the one beside her, which was already plated. I noticed the seat across from me also had a plate, which had already been used, and wondered who had been here before me, but didn't dare ask.

"Ronald, please bring out some breakfast for Mademoiselle Joslyn. I'm sure she's famished after last night's celebrations."

"Did you enjoy yourself?" I asked. "I didn't get a chance to speak to you."

"Of course not. You were busy. Busy with the wedding, the guests . . . my son."

I reached for the water set in front of me and drank some, hoping it would help extinguish the furious blush spreading over my face. "I was quite busy," I said once I set the glass down.

"So, tell me about this little charade you and my son have going." She said it so flippantly, I had no choice but to look her in the eye. *Had Aramis come clean about it to her? After everything he'd said to me? After telling me not to tell a soul? As if reading my thoughts, she smiled slightly. "My son told me it was all for show."

"Oh."

"He didn't give me many details beyond that." She reached for the newspaper folded up in front of her plate and unfolded it, showing me the front page. There was a photograph of Pilar and Ben kissing after they said their vows and beneath it, one of Aramis and me kissing in the hall. "Whose idea was this?"

"His. I told him to let me handle the press, but he went behind my back and staged the photograph. He said it was best to get the news out there as soon as possible."

"My son can be a bit much. As you know."

"I'm definitely aware." I sighed, thanking the butler when he set the already plated breakfast in front of me. I dug in slowly, knowing the Queen Mother's eyes were on me and that she'd start talking any minute.

"He said it didn't work out with Cassandra of Greece."

"He finds a flaw in everyone." I shook my head.

"Except for you."

"Me?" I coughed and reached for the water once again, grateful that I didn't have food in my mouth when she said that. "He has always been keen to point out my flaws."

"Because he likes you. Genuinely."

"If that's what he does to people he genuinely likes, I'm glad I don't have him as an enemy." I set the glass down and raised an eyebrow at her. "He seems to think if he didn't have a girlfriend right now the press was going to have him under a magnifying glass."

"But now they'll have you both under that magnifying glass," she said. "Did you consider that before you agreed to this?"

"No." I felt myself frown. "Not really."

"What are you expecting to happen?" She watched me closely. I was no longer hungry enough to eat anything because now I felt like I was under attack.

"With what?"

"With all of this. We gave you an opportunity on our

staff. We gave you more responsibility than you originally signed up for. Now you're dating my son, or rather, pretending to date him. You'll parade around with him in public and take photos. Was this your plan all along? To become famous and then . . . and then what? What will you achieve?"

"That was not my plan. He came up with the whole thing. He basically bribed me to do it. He even asked me not to tell anyone that it was all for show, so imagine my surprise at the fact that you know what's happening."

"My son doesn't keep secrets from me. However, I can assure you he definitely keeps them from you. My best advice is not to get invested in this. Aramis won't settle down."

"I'm not planning on getting invested."

"Good. Then I guess that's settled."

My stomach rolled. I suddenly wasn't feeling so good. I took a deep breath before addressing her again. "Was that why you wanted to speak to me? To tell me not to get invested?"

"I wanted to try to understand why my son would choose someone on our payroll to pretend to be in love with when he could very well have chosen an heiress or socialite to do it with. Cassandra of Greece is high on my list of women for him to marry. She's a suitable choice, don't you agree?"

I swallowed the bile rising in my throat and nodded. "She checks all the boxes."

"The car accident he suffered left him feeling less than," she mused. "That's the only possible explanation as to why he's doing this. Of the three of them, he was the one with the best potential for a wife and he's throwing that away and wasting his time. Your time as well. You should consider that you're not getting any younger. If you want to find a suitable man to marry, you need to do it soon."

"That's not high on my list of things to do."

"What is?"

"I figured I was doing a fine job as it is, working for your family."

"Yes, but now we have to consider hiring a new secretary as I'm sure you'll be busy with Aramis attending any event the King may have lined up for him."

"I do that anyway. I've been doing that since the accident and I've still been able to consult Pilar and help Adeline when needed."

"Queen Adeline." The Queen Mother raised an eyebrow. "Don't forget your place." She took the folded newspaper and stood. "I'm sure I'll be seeing you around."

I felt as though she'd slapped me, but stood and curtsied once more before letting myself fall back into the chair. She'd always liked me. I swore she did, but everything she'd just told me felt like the complete opposite of someone who liked and respected me.

CHAPTER TWENTY-THREE

ARAMIS

I WASN'T SURE WHAT CHANGED BETWEEN LAST NIGHT AND THIS morning, or if it was general regret for what transpired last night, now that we were forced to take a look at everything in the light of day, but Joslyn was acting strange. I'd asked her to accompany me to two places today—I had to take Oscar back to his mother's house and was slated to feed the less fortunate later this afternoon alongside Addie and Elias. Pilar and Ben were away on their mini-honeymoon, and it was my job to take their place. I figured, since the world knew about me and Joslyn, why not give them a show? Besides, she loved participating in things like that normally. Why not make it official? Well, the why not had her arms crossed, staring out the window during our ride to Oscar's mother's house. Oscar was playing with action figures from the wedding reception that he got to keep, and I was too busy trying to figure out her mood. Augustus, the butler, told me she had breakfast with my mother, which was odd considering I'd had breakfast with my mother and she never ate twice in a row. They spoke often though. My mother liked to be kept aware of things. I chalked it up to that. Still, I didn't understand why Joslyn was being short with me. Unless she regretted last night. And fuck, the reality of that hurt more than I cared to admit.

Last night I'd lay myself bare for her. Literally. Something I hadn't done since before the accident. Something I wasn't sure I wanted to do again with anyone else. That was what struck me most about all of this. I loved playing the field. I loved being with different women. I loved not having to answer to anyone. Maybe that was the issue with all of this. Those were things I once loved, but no longer wanted. The realization hit me like a ton of bricks. I stopped looking at Joslyn and instead looked outside of the window beside me as the driver continued down the winding path that led to Oscar's house. Whatever awaited there was another thing to prepare for.

CHAPTER TWENTY-FOUR

JOSLYN

I'D BEEN IN THE SITTING AREA OF ESMÉE'S HOUSE FOR TWENTY minutes now, while Oscar and Aramis visited with her. The ride over had been uncomfortable, to say the least. I kept replaying my conversation with Aramis's mother and coming to the same conclusion. The Queen Mother did not approve of our relationship, fake or otherwise. To make matters worse, she'd made me feel like a commoner, which I was, of course. I knew that, of course, but in the years I'd known her she'd always made me feel welcome, like family. It was a far cry from what was happening now. I tried to think back to when Elias and Adeline started dating and how she treated Addie, but as far as I remember, she'd always been nice to her. Maybe the King desperately needed a wife and wasn't willing to play his mother's game of *Find an Aristocrat*. All along, Aramis had been bedding them, so who was to say she didn't think there was a chance he'd marry one and restore balance to The Crown once more. After all, how strong was a Crown made up of commoners?

I tried to picture the Queen Mother visiting this home, as they said she did often, to see her grandson and make sure he was well taken care of. Had she sat on these white couches? The house itself was very quaint, but adorable, and Esmée had it decorated with a very minimal style, though there were photographs of Oscar and their family hanging on the walls and over the mantle and as it was Christmas, it looked like a reindeer had barged in and proceeded to throw up in here. The house felt nothing like one of The Crown's lavishly decorated places, and even though I was curious to meet the woman behind the light décor, and Oscar's well-mannered upbringing, upon walking inside I quickly announced I'd wait here. It wasn't that I was jealous of her, the poor girl was bedridden after suffering a fall in which she'd been decorating this very house. I just . . . I wasn't sure how to feel about someone who held such an important role in Aramis's life, albeit it being a newly important role. I was still lost in thought when Oscar ran back into the room.

"Maman wants to meet you."

"Me?" I stood up, eyes wide.

"She says she wants to see who I've been spending time with," he said. "Papa says you should meet."

"Okay. I'll follow you then."

Oscar turned and grabbed my hand, escorting me down the hall. My heart pounded with each step. I hadn't bothered to ask what exactly went wrong with Esmée after the great fall or what exactly she'd been standing on that caused it. I'd merely kept quiet each time she was brought up, and when it was Oscar speaking about her, I smiled, because with the way his eyes lit up at the mention of her, I had no choice but to. I knew when we reached the door to the room she was in, because he squeezed my hand and gave a little excited squeal as he pushed open the door. I wasn't sure what I was expecting, but not high on that list was not catching a glimpse of Aramis standing over a woman's bed and fluffing her pillow whilst she gazed up lovingly at him. He didn't even budge when he caught me by the door. She didn't even look my way at all, just continued to stare up at this literal Prince who was obviously here to save her, or at least help her. When he finally, slowly, separated himself from her bed, Esmée glanced over at me with a soft, kind smile on her face.

"Please, come in," she said. "I've been looking forward to meeting you."

My heart was hammering too loudly—in my throat, in my ears, through my veins—for me to respond, so I tried as hard as I could to collect myself and smile with a small nod instead. What could I say? I instantly hated her. Before,

I hadn't been jealous. I'd made it a point not to think about her at all, but now she was here and she was real and she had his attention and was linked to him for life and I hated her. Hated that she'd been the only one he hadn't used protection with, or so he claimed. Hated that he was so adamant in using it with me, which was an absolute shit thought, considering I wouldn't have let him go without it, but it was the principle of it all. I stood at the foot of the bed as Oscar let go of my hand and climbed on it, sitting by her feet.

"This is Joslyn. She takes care of me and gave me all the toys I showed you. She plans weddings. Big ones like the Princess had last night."

"Hello, Joslyn." She smiled. "I'm Esmée. Thank you for taking care of my son. He's told me a lot about you."

"It's been great to get to know him." I looked at Oscar and suddenly my smile wasn't forced. "How are you feeling? I heard you had a pretty big fall."

"Big is one way to put it." She laughed lightly. "I fractured my skull, broke my arm, sprained an ankle. I'm just grateful to be alive."

"We're all grateful you're alive," Aramis added and my eyes gravitated toward him.

He was serious. It wasn't one of his fabricated comments he used in front of most people. I was taken aback by all of it. Too taken aback to begin to process why I even cared this much.

"I'm going to get my Hulk toy." Oscar hopped off the bed and ran out.

"He's so full of energy," I said with a smile, looking at the door.

"So, I heard you're in a pretend relationship with Aramis. How is that going so far?"

I blinked, my head whipping in her direction as my mouth dropped, but recovered quickly, shrugging a shoulder and taking a painful swallow of my emotions. He'd told her it was fake? We were hiding this from my family, his brother, his sister, his sister-in-law, both of whom were my best friends, and he'd told his mother and now Esmée? His mother, I understood. I set that one aside while I was in the sitting area, knowing how meddlesome the Queen Mother could be with her children, but Esmée? What was the purpose of him telling her?

"Joss." That was Aramis, shooting me a puzzled look. "How is it going so far?"

"Pretending? Fine. Easy. I mean, Aramis and I are practically brother and sister at this point." I smiled wide enough to show all my teeth. A grin, or grimace, I wasn't sure.

"Yes, he tells me you've known each other most of your lives."

"We have." I kept smiling. He'd told her a lot of things it seemed. "It's nice to see you two getting along after not being in each other's lives for so long."

"It has been nice." Esmée glanced over at Aramis. I could feel his eyes on me, but didn't dare look at him out of fear that I'd punch him. "He calls every day, visits every other day, spends hours here talking about life. It really has been amazing."

"Wow," I said again because I had nothing articulate to add to that. "That's more than he does for his brother these days, but I'm sure you know that."

"Oh, brothers are always there for each other, that's the beauty of it. The King is busy and Aramis has his own life. He has a son and now another family to spend time with."

"How lucky for him." I swallowed again and looked at my watch. "We should get going, Aramis. The King and Queen are waiting for us. I could take the car first and send it back over to pick you up if you wish."

"No, it's fine, I'll ride with you." He stood, setting a hand over Esmée's. "I'll be back this weekend to pick up Oscar."

"I look forward to seeing you. Maybe by then I'll be out of this bed and ready to walk around with you."

"Take it easy, Esmée. Only do as much as you have to. You have around-the-clock staff for a reason." He shot her a look as he stepped away from the bed and walked over.

"It was nice meeting you, Joslyn. Meeting you has solidified everything my son told me and has made me realize just how much I love the loyal royal staff." She smiled.

"It was nice meeting you as well." I walked out of the room before my face contorted into anything less than pleasant. The way she spoke to me was reminiscent of the

Queen Mother's conversation this morning. Maybe that was why the two got along so well. They felt everyone else was just here to merely entertain and serve them.

"You're leaving?" Oscar asked when I reached him. He was sitting at the dinner table with an older man, his grandfather, I assumed.

"Yes, but I'll see you in a few days."

"Okay. Thanks for the toys," he said with a grin and a sparkle in his green eyes that matched his father's.

"You're welcome."

Aramis was on my heels, but stayed to say goodbye to his son while I walked outside. Pierre was there to open the back door of the SUV. For a moment, even after he settled into the driver's seat, we were silent.

"So, how was it?" he asked. I met his gaze in the rearview.

"It was fine."

"Your face is tomato-red. I'd say you're not doing fine."

"It was awful," I said honestly. Pierre and I were friends. He was more part of this family than some of its members. He offered a small smile.

"It can't be easy meeting your boyfriend's . . . baby's mother?" He frowned slightly. "At least you know you have nothing to worry about."

"I wouldn't be so sure." I looked back at the white house. "She's pretty, nice, talks very much like his mother, despite not being an aristocrat."

Pierre chuckled. "Well, then, you definitely have

nothing to worry about. Aramis would never marry a woman who reminds him of his mother."

"I think you're confusing brothers." I raised an eyebrow. "Elias, sure, he went off and found himself a commoner with sense and style and grace."

"All things the Queen Mother doesn't have?" Pierre raised his own eyebrow.

"You seem to want them to cut off my tongue."

"They don't do that anymore," he quipped.

"Allegedly," I added, and he said at the same time.

We both laughed. I felt my body temperature lower back to an acceptable degree and suddenly felt at ease. Maybe the issue wasn't Aramis or Esmée. This was on me. I'd been hired to do a job and pretending to be with him was part of that job. Work is work. You don't have to love it, you just have to get it done. That was how I needed to look at this situation, but when I saw Aramis walk out of that house, looking gorgeous in his winter clothing, I wasn't sure I could stop being angry enough to remember that.

CHAPTER TWENTY-FIVE

ARAMIS

Once again, she didn't say a word to me in the car on our way to the community center. I sat in the front with Pierre. There was no use in sitting beside a person who obviously didn't want anything to do with you, even if it was the person you were willing to give up everything for. Of course, Joslyn didn't know that and I wasn't sure I'd tell her today. I'd planned on doing it today. After speaking to my mother this morning, I came to the realization that this pretend stuff was bullshit. You couldn't pretend what we experienced last night. I couldn't help but shake my head at that thought. Me, of all people, complicating sex with emotions. This was Joslyn though. I felt like I'd known her my entire life, even though we'd met when she and my sister were teenagers, and I was the slightly older brother who was addicted to partying and popping pills. That summer, when Pilar brought Joslyn along to Versailles for a holiday, it felt like fate, kismet. From the moment our eyes met, I felt the spark. It was the very spark I'd kept hidden under countless jokes. I wasn't ready for commitment back then or in the years that followed. I enjoyed the party, enjoyed being the center of attention, enjoyed the tabloid rumors, but things had changed quickly for me since the accident. Since Oscar. Things were still shaky with my mother, who was doing everything in her power to repair our relationship, but it was difficult. I'd lost seven years of my son's life, and for what? It was something I'd spoken to Esmée about today. I was ready to go on record about my son, to accept him publicly and let the world know how proud I was to be his father. Esmée wasn't so sure. She'd managed to live under the radar all these years, managed to dodge the tabloids. It was yet another thing I needed to speak to Joslyn about since she was in charge of putting out statements. When I saw that we were nearing the community house, I took a breath and turned around to see her typing furiously on her cell phone.

Who was she texting? David? The thought felt like a crushing blow to my ego. As if sensing my eyes on her, she glanced up, but I could tell she meant to look right back down at the screen. It was probably David. Fucking David. I swallowed.

"Yes?" She raised an eyebrow.

"I need you to put out a statement on behalf of Esmée and myself about Oscar."

"What would you like it to say?" She looked at the screen again.

"Isn't figuring it out your job?"

"It seems impersonal to have the papers announce it." She met my eyes again. She looked annoyed by me, or this, or both. "You should do this with a camera. Broadcast it. Share it on social media. We can record it ourselves so you don't have to involve the press directly if you'd like. Either way, we need to run this by the King before we do anything."

"You know my brother will want the press involved."

"I guess we'll find out soon." She looked outside the front windshield.

I turned and did the same. My brother and Adeline's caravan had already gotten here and the two of them were walking toward the center, shaking hands with people and smiling at cameras. My brother was truly a people's King. It was why he always had media attention. He hadn't always been like that. There was a time my brother saw a camera and ran the other way. My parents would talk about how he wasn't ready for the role, but I couldn't imagine anyone better.

Once inside, we greeted my brother and Adeline in the backroom, where we were given aprons to put over our clothes. We were all dressed in jeans and T-shirts, but we put the aprons on anyway. Adeline and Joslyn walked to the front first, and my brother made to follow, but I stopped him.

"I have to talk to you about something."

"Is it about your little meeting with Mother this morning?" He was still fidgeting with the tie on his apron, which was slightly ripped and kept coming undone.

"I didn't have a little meeting with Mother, I had breakfast with her. You could have joined."

"I have breakfast with her often. I don't need to join yours. I assumed you had a lot to talk about." He shrugged a shoulder. "So, is all forgiven?"

"I can't stay mad at her forever."

"You always have been her favorite." Elias smiled when he said it. It was somewhere between a truth and an exaggeration. Everyone always said I was our mother's favorite, though I couldn't imagine why. Elias was her first born and Pilar was the baby, and the perfect daughter.

"I can't imagine she'd keep a secret this big from her favorite child for seven years," I said. A reminder that punched me in the gut whenever I thought of it.

"Your first mistake, then, was thinking she cared about any of us more than she cared about The Crown." Elias raised an eyebrow. "What did you need to speak to me about? We should be getting out there soon." He looked at the door.

"Joslyn."

"What about her?"

"I wanted her to put out a statement about Oscar and Esmée. I don't want to keep my son a secret from the world."

"I agree with that. It would feel more genuine if you did it in front of a camera. You're charismatic. They love you. They've forgiven all of your missteps."

"Missteps?"

"Like doing cocaine on top of tables in clubs." He shot me an amused look. "Or taking home every single woman you could and kicking them out of your apartment."

"I don't do those things anymore."

"I've noticed. I don't know if it was Oscar who brought upon the change, or Joslyn, or the accident, but I'm glad you're taking care of yourself now."

I gave a nod, feeling a lump in my throat as I took in what he'd said. He wasn't wrong. I'd been reckless for years. Between my absolute need for attention and acceptance and being in the wrong group of friends, I'd been going down the wrong path fast. The accident definitely triggered the change. Starting with the realization that I'd survived it and others didn't and continuing with the headlines of my unworthiness. Add to that, my friends didn't even care to visit me in the hospital or ask how I was doing in physical therapy after my surgeries. They only showed up afterwards, when I started with the parties again, pretending I was fine, that everything was fine. Joslyn saw through it though. She showed up every night, cleaned up after me, helped me to bed, helped me pack, helped me

with my schedule and went to all the events to make sure I showed up. She did a lot more than clean up my image. She helped clean me up and that was worth more than gold to me, to my brother, to The Crown.

"Let Joslyn set up the television interview. She knows what she's doing." Elias set a hand on my shoulder and squeezed. "Let's go out there now."

CHAPTER TWENTY-SIX

JOSLYN

WAS GREAT AT MY JOB, BUT I WASN'T AN ACTRESS, AND I WAS tired of pretending. I'd stood alongside Aramis, smiling at everyone who walked up to us and serving their food. I watched as King Elias and Queen Adeline spoke to each person with genuine interest and affection. It was fine, picture perfect, until they asked Aramis about our relationship and he said, "What can I say? Sometimes love is right underneath our noses." He'd kissed me right after saying the words, too, as if to drive the notion home. As if he meant it, and it nearly brought me to tears. I hated it. I hated him for doing this to me and myself for caring this deeply for a man who would never, ever, return my feelings. I hated that I let myself get in this deep. We were supposed to be fooling everyone, not each other, and definitely not ourselves. By the time we left the center, I felt defeated, depleted, even. I'd already been through the motions at Esmée's house. I'd been through the motions in the car, thinking about how the interview would fare when Aramis introduced the world to Oscar and Esmée. I'd been through the motions in the center with each set of eyes that landed on us and each smile I gave in front of the camera, knowing they were always watching. I promised myself that in the car I could let my guard down. In my car, I could let go of all of this tension. And so, instead of walking to the car Pierre was driving, which had brought Aramis and me, I went to one of the others in the caravan and asked them to take me back to Versailles alone. I'd gotten Adeline's approval, of course. She didn't know what was going on with me, but she knew me well enough to know I needed space.

Once in the car, I got an email from King Elias's secretary, John, with some journalists who would love to interview Aramis and would put a good spin on this story. Instead of spending time alone with my feelings, I spent it vetting the journalists and emailing one—a charming journalist who was a father of five and known to put the royal family on a pedestal. Once that was done, we were already nearing the palace, so I took the remaining moments alone to close my eyes and say a chant to myself: he was never mine to lose. He wasn't. If he wanted to bring Esmée into his life as my replacement and as a real relationship, that was absolutely his right. Who was I to put a stop to that? No one. A measly commoner. A lowly secretary on their payroll and in their staff. It didn't matter that the Princess and Queen were my best friends. The fact remained that I was not Oscar's mother, who had lifelong ties to Aramis and according to his mother, I was not a choice for him to marry.

"Ma'am, we're here." The driver set the car in park.

I opened my eyes and looked out the window. It had started to snow. Light, but white tiny specs were clinging to the window. I smiled at the sight. Much like love and heartbreak, the cold could be grueling, but it brought beautiful treasures. I stepped out of the car, shutting my coat tightly over myself as I walked toward the cottages. I was hungry and tired and would absolutely be calling the main house tonight for my food. It was something I didn't often do, since I liked spending time with my friends in the main areas, but I wasn't up for it tonight. When I turned the key to my cottage, I looked toward Aramis's cottage and saw him walking toward me. Instead of waiting, I opened the door and stepped inside, shutting it behind me and locking it for good measure. My heart was pounding as I pressed against it. The knock I knew was coming fell over the door on the other side, but even then, I ignored it.

"Joss. I want to speak to you. I know you're standing right there," he said.

I was annoyed at the fact that he was so confident

in my being there, and even more annoyed at him insisting I open the door. I decided to ignore him. Let him keep knocking. I kicked off my boots and walked toward the room, shutting and locking that door as well. I called the main house and asked them to bring my dinner and to please wait thirty minutes since I was about to get into the shower. The person on the other line was friendly and agreed, the way we all do when working for The Crown. I showered, taking my time under the spray to shut my eyes and collect my thoughts, my breath, my emotions. It didn't work. When I stepped out, I felt just as lost as I had when I'd walked in there, but at least I was calm and clean. I dried my hair quickly, running my fingers through it as the heat of the dryer hit it, and dressed in a comfortable long-sleeve T-shirt dress and long cotton socks. When I opened the door, a young girl walked inside, placed everything on the table, and walked back out letting me know she'd be back in two hours to collect everything. I thanked her and shut the door upon her departure before rushing over to the food and wine. Tonight, I'd have food and wine and binge-watch a gossipy drama. The only kind of excitement I was welcoming in my life was that of a person on the screen.

CHAPTER TWENTY-SEVEN

ARAMIS

ADELINE WAS THE ONLY THING BETWEEN ME AND JOSLYN tonight. First, she'd asked me to walk to the main house with her. Then, she'd poured me and Elias some whiskey. Then, she made us finish putting up the Christmas decorations in the library, as if anyone ever walked in here. Forget the fact that the entire palace looked like St. Nicholas's workshop and all of our staff had done a marvelous job decorating it. Adeline wanted us to do some of the work. Something we'd never done in . . . ever. I blamed it on her American upbringing. She'd spent entirely too much time over there. First with the football love and now with the desire to make us do all of this work as a

way to spend time with us. As if we didn't spend enough time together already. Still, no one says no to the Queen, especially not while she's pregnant and moody. I wasn't sure if she was doing this because she knew that once the baby arrived things would change or if she was doing it so I wouldn't show up on Joslyn's doorstep tonight. She told her something. I saw the two of them whispering back and forth before Joss got in a car by herself and headed back over. The most words I'd gotten out of her today were in an email, letting me know we had a televised interview scheduled for tomorrow night.

She'd also already told one of the wardrobe people on our staff to make sure Esmée and Oscar looked impeccable for the interview. Esmée was mostly fine now, aside from the cast on her leg and the brace on her arm. Her face was unmarred and the bandage on her head had been removed. It was something we'd bonded over, the accidents. Her fall had left her questioning everything, including her ability to be a single mother, something I assured her she'd done a great job with. It was more than that. Anything that made you face your mortality head-on like that changed you in too many ways to count. It was something Esmée understood as well as I did. It was the reason she'd sent Oscar to me in the first place. She knew my mother never told me about him and didn't feel comfortable hiding any of it anymore.

"You're lost in thought." That was Adeline. I blinked and met her eyes. "It's your move."

I moved a pawn forward on the chessboard between us.

"Are you nervous about the interview tomorrow?" She moved the horse she had left.

"Not really. I feel like I've been ready to talk about him to the world since I met him." I smiled at that.

"You're a proud father," Elias said from across the room. He was reading a book and sipping on whiskey. "As you should be. He's a great kid."

"Soon enough he'll have a cousin to play with," I said, continuing the game even though I knew Adeline would beat me. She always did. "Do you think you'll make it to full-term?"

"Full-term is December 24th. That's next week. I'm not sure, but then again, I didn't think I'd make it to this week." She sighed heavily. "I'm so uncomfortable. My back hurts. My ribs hurt. I can't sleep. I need to use the toilet every five seconds."

"She's miserable," Elias added loudly. "We're all miserable. The little prince needs to hurry up and get here already."

"You look great." I shrugged a shoulder. "And the fact that you're still making appearances is impressive."

"She looks and acts the way a Queen is supposed to." We all turned to see my mother walking into the library.

"Mother," I said.

"Mother," Elias said.

"Madame," Adeline added with a smile. "Care to join us?"

"Have you already beat him?" my mother asked.

"Not yet. I'm taking it easy on him tonight. He seems distracted."

My mother sat down in the chair beside us. I was surprised to see her dressed down, in wide white pants and a light purple sweater. She wasn't even wearing heels tonight and her hair was swept into a low bun. She was dressed very similar to Addie tonight.

"It's too bad we can't share a bottle of wine," my mother said.

"Soon. Hopefully soon." Addie groaned. "I'm ready to have this baby already."

"Have you settled on Louis?"

"I think so." Addie smiled. "Prince Louis has a nice ring to it."

"It's a good homage to the French," Mother said.

"Prince Louis Amadeo," Addie said.

Mother gasped, setting a hand on her chest. "Really?"

"Really." Addie smiled.

"It does have a nice ring to it, doesn't it?" Elias asked, walking over to us. He set a hand on his wife's shoulder.

"It's beautiful." My mother smiled, her eyes glazing. "My father, may he rest in peace, would be so happy. So happy."

"It's a good homage to the French and Spanish," I said. "Dammit."

"Check," Addie said.

"Fuck. I knew I should have taken your queen."

"She's good with the queens," Elias said.

My mother laughed. I shook my head.

"What does Joslyn say about tomorrow's interview?" My mother asked as I tried to figure out my next move.

"She set it up."

"She loves you. You know that, right?" my mother asked.

"She's . . ." I looked at Addie, Elias, and back at my mother. Neither my brother nor my sister-in-law knew that all of this was pretend. Now it felt dumb to hide it. "She doesn't love me. She's just going along with this because she has to."

"Joss doesn't go along with anything because she has to." Addie laughed. "Checkmate. I think you're done. I have you cornered."

"I kind of . . . talked her into pretending she was my girlfriend," I said, feeling like I was betraying Joslyn by telling her best friend before she did, but I really did feel cornered now. Cornered by this conversation and my growing emotions. I was out of my element here.

"Hm." It was the only thing Addie said.

I looked at my brother and knew he wanted to say something but didn't dare say it in front of his wife. Who knew what he was thinking. My mother merely sat there, staring at the pieces on the chessboard, the way she often did.

"What does that mean?" I knocked over my king, who was screwed either way he went.

"Maybe it feels like you're pretending, but I'm not sure she does," Addie said.

"That's the thing, I don't . . . I'm not pretending. I'm . . . " I took a breath. Why was it so difficult to say these things aloud? "I don't know if I'm falling for her now or if I've always felt this way about her, but I'm definitely not pretending and I don't know what to do about it."

"Tell her how you feel," my mother said.

"It's not that simple."

"It actually is that simple," my brother said.

"Look who's talking." I shot him a look. "How long did it take you to tell Addie anything?"

"That was different. My entire life has been shaped for me to marry an aristocrat and I knew it was going to be a challenge. That's not expected of you. Pilar married a regular guy. I mean, he's famous and he's worshipped and idolized because he's arguably the best footballer in the world, but still, regular guy."

"Wow. For a moment I thought you were going to profess your love to Ben," Addie said, making us laugh. When she got serious, she said, "I think the issue is that because the King married a commoner and the Princess married a commoner, you probably think you need to do the opposite to salvage a lifelong tradition. Am I right?"

"Sort of." I glanced at my mother, who was smiling.

"You think I care," my mother said, still smiling.

"Don't you?"

"I care that you went behind my back and went after Joslyn after I distinctly remember telling you not to." She raised an eyebrow. "Not only is she our preferred secretary, but she's also your sister's best friend and practically family. This relationship with her could ruin all of that."

"It won't. I would never do anything to hurt her."

"Meaning you're going to marry her?" Mother asked.

"I didn't say that."

"That's the only thing you could do to potentially 'not hurt her,'" she emphasized.

"What?" I blinked. "When did marriage become part of this?"

"I'm not saying you have to marry her. I'm telling you that it would make her feel secure in the relationship if you showed her that you're serious about her." My mother tilted her head slightly. "Besides, you know the question will start to come up soon enough."

"It'll definitely be on everyone's mind at our gala," Elias added.

"I don't care if I'm asked about marriage. I don't have to answer to anyone about my relationships, especially not one that I'm actually serious about."

"She doesn't even know you're serious about it," my brother said.

"Well, she will. I'll tell her I'm serious." I glanced at my watch and sent her a text to see if she was still awake.

"She has a long day ahead of her tomorrow," Addie said. "In the morning, she's running errands with me and then we have your interview to attend. You'll have to tell her afterwards."

"I'm perfectly capable of figuring out when I'm going to tell her." I scowled.

"I know." Addie smiled. "I just want to give you a heads-up in case you were considering telling her before the interview."

"Thanks for the tip." I glanced at my phone again and saw no response from Joslyn.

Dammit. I wish I'd thought to get a key to her room before. I would kill to sleep in her bed tonight. Just sleep. The thought sobered me up. I set my whiskey down. I was definitely in love with her. One hundred percent, without a doubt.

CHAPTER TWENTY-EIGHT

JOSLYN

My head was pounding, but I managed to make my way to the car that was waiting to take Adeline and me away. She wanted to get a gift for Elias for when the baby arrived—a watch engraved with the baby's name, which would later also have his birth date and time. It was a ridiculous gesture, in my opinion. She was the one who grew a human and would be pushing him out of her vagina. If anyone deserved a present, it was her. I wasn't going to tell her that though. If she wanted to get him something for this, that was on her. Besides, we were also going to look for dresses for the Christmas gala and that was the kind of shopping I could get behind. She smiled when I stepped into the car with a shiver.

"It's cold today."

"I know. I asked Thomas to get more space heaters for the gala because of it," she said.

"I got them," Thomas said from the front seat.

"Should I go to the jeweler first or the designer?" Pierre asked.

"Jeweler, please," Addie said, then turned to me. "Did you sleep well?"

"I did, but woke up with a massive headache. Maybe it was the wine, even though I didn't have much of it. I think I fell asleep at eight. I can't remember the last time that happened."

"That is early." She frowned. "Are you feeling okay?"

"Just tired." And emotionally drained.

"I had an interesting conversation with Aramis last night."

"Oh?" My heart pounded. "What about?"

"You, mostly."

"What did he say?" I swallowed.

"That this relationship is all pretend." She eyed me closely.

"I'm sorry I didn't tell you. I should have." I felt my face grow hot and my eyes water. He'd told my best friend about us without consulting me? I wasn't sure what hurt more. That or the fact that he truly didn't feel anything for me.

"I don't care." She set a hand on mine. "Just be careful, Joss. And speak to him. I know you both and I know how much you like to keep your feelings bottled up. I don't think it's a good idea in this case."

"What am I supposed to tell him? That I have feelings for him? That I don't want to pretend anymore?"

"Yes."

"I can't." I shook my head. "He'll just make a joke out of it. Or call the whole thing off."

"I don't think he will do either of those things."

"The Queen Mother is against it."

"She told you that?" Addie raised an eyebrow.

"Not in those words, but basically she made it very clear that I was staff."

"That's because you're the best at your job." She shot a look toward the front seat. "No offense, Thomas."

"None taken, Your Royal Highness."

"So cheeky." Addie rolled her eyes with a smile.

The only time she let anyone on the staff refer to her as Your Royal Highness was when they were in public. Everyone knew that saying that in private made her uncomfortable.

"It wasn't like that," I said. "She was telling me to know my place."

"She refers to you as family."

"And now staff."

"Joslyn." Adeline sighed heavily. "Please don't get in your feelings about this."

"Why not? My feelings are valid."

"I'm not saying they're not. I would never say that,

but you have the tendency to exaggerate at times and this may be one of those times."

"It's not." I crossed my arms and looked out of the car. "Do you know how difficult it is to plan an interview for a man you have feelings for and his son's mother? Whom he just met, by the way." I looked at her again. "He had no recollection of this girl whatsoever, and now they're . . . you should see them." I sighed, shaking my head. "It's like they've known each other their whole lives. The way he takes care of her and the way she looks at him like he walks on water." My stomach churned at the memory.

"You're jealous."

"I am."

"You have every right to be, but it's not her he wants. It's you."

"He said that?"

"Basically." She shrugged a shoulder, smiling. Butterflies swarmed my stomach. "Just, please, talk to him."

"Okay." I smiled back.

"Well, you two were gone a long time," the Queen Mother said upon seeing us. "I want to see what you got for the gala."

"Adeline got the most gorgeous, flowy, Valentino dress," I said. "It's a dream."

"And you?"

"Also a Valentino, but more of a classic, black, long dress."

"With the most exquisite exposed back," Adeline said. "We would have invited you to come with, but I know you had a breakfast scheduled this morning."

"With Esmée, yes." The Queen Mother smiled. My heart dropped into the pit of my stomach. "I just wanted to prepare her for the questions."

"Is the journalist setting up?" I asked, ignoring the pang in my chest.

"He's ready to go. Will you grab my son? He's in his cottage. Oscar is running around with Rose."

"I'll get him now." I curtsied to both of them and walked outside, to my cottage first to drop off my garment bag and shoes, and then straight to Aramis's cottage. My heart pounded hard against my chest as I approached and knocked. He opened the door, his eyes widening when he saw me.

"Joslyn."

"Everyone is waiting for you in the main house." I was surprised at how casual and business-like I sounded with the butterflies swarming all over. He looked ridiculously handsome, with his dark hair brushed back, light beard on his face, those eyes that could melt an iceberg.

"Come in. I'm almost finished getting ready." He held the door open for me. I froze. "I won't bite. Unless you want me to." He chuckled. My stomach flipped again.

"Stop saying things like that," I whisper-shouted as I stepped inside.

"I've been saying things like that for years. You never seemed to mind." He shut the door behind me.

I kept my back to him, but heard his footsteps as he closed the distance between us, felt the warmth of his body behind mine, and when he wrapped an arm around my waist and pulled me flush against his chest, I couldn't help the moan that escaped my lips.

"Is it because now that I've done it, you can't stop thinking about it?" His voice was a murmur against the back of my neck. He swept my hair to one side and kissed my axis, awakening every single nerve and shooting a shiver down my spine. "Is it because you long for me the way I long for you?" He kissed the side of my neck and moved my shirt to suck on my shoulder.

"Please don't, Aramis. Not right now," I whispered.

There were tears in my eyes I couldn't help and they had nothing to do with happiness or sadness. It was pure lust. A burn in my eyes I couldn't help. Ever since he text messaged me last night the only thing I could think about was the next time we'd have sex and we had no time for this, not right now.

"I want you, Joslyn. I want you naked, I want you

wet, I want you on my cock." He continued murmuring these words as he kissed the other side of my neck. "Tell me you don't want me too."

"I do." It was a guttural cry. "We don't have time right now."

"Take off your clothes."

"We don't have time." I turned in his arms. "I'm serious."

"Take off your pants. We can be quick."

I kicked off my boots and undid my pants, pulling them down quickly. He pulled his down as well. Our lips crashed against each other's, our tongues exploring, our mouths desperate. His hand scooped into my panties, his fingers not giving warning before he pumped them inside of me with a growl.

"You're wet," he said against my lips. "So fucking wet for me."

"Just fuck me. Please." I finished kicking off my jeans as he lowered my panties and continued to finger me, his thumb on my clit, three of his fingers inside of me, pleasuring me in a way that was driving my eyes to roll back. When he pulled them out, it was to lift up my ass and slam me against the wall, his fingers replaced by his cock, hard and stretching me.

"Fuck, Joslyn." He stopped for a second, letting me acclimate, opening me up to his girth as he pulled me down onto him.

"Condom," I gasped. "Condom."

"Papers." He signaled at the table beside us. "Clean. Everything is clean. You said—"

I silenced him with a hard kiss. He pumped into me. I wanted to cry, he felt so good. "Fuck me, Aramis."

He didn't say another word, just drove into me as he pulled me up and down onto his cock. All I could do was hold on to his shoulders and squeeze as he moved inside of me. My head fell back, leaving my neck exposed to his mouth, sucking as he fucked me in relentless motions—hard and fast, as if he couldn't last another second without being inside of me. I came hard, so hard, and knew he felt it because he groaned deeply, in a way that made me come once more. My body shook, my legs giving out even though I wasn't using them. He gripped my ass so tight as he came inside of me, I wasn't sure I'd be able to walk or see straight for days. We were both breathing heavily when our eyes met again. His searched mine and I thought he was going to say something, anything, but instead, he kissed me. It was the sweetest, softest kiss, and when he pulled away, he reached over for a towel and set it between my legs as he pulled out of me. I held on to it as my feet shakily hit the floor.

"Now I'm ready for the camera." He grinned at me and winked. My heart stuttered.

"Can we talk?" I asked. "Afterwards, I mean."

"Sure. I think Esmée and Oscar are staying for lunch, but we can speak after they're gone."

"I'd like that." I smiled as I watched him get dressed again.

I was ready to clear the air, and I had a feeling Addie was right. Aramis and I were on the same page about our feelings. One of us just needed to come out and outright say it and I decided it would be me.

CHAPTER TWENTY-NINE

I WATCHED AS OSCAR HELD HIS BATMAN ACTION FIGURE IN his hands and sat between his parents. He was so adorable and I had no doubt the public would go crazy over him. Esmée looked beautiful as well, in an ivory dress with a conservative scoop neck. Aramis was wearing a black shirt with a high collar, a style he loved to wear these days, probably to conceal burns from the car accident.

"So, you have some pretty big news," the interviewer started.

"I'd say finding out I have a son is probably the biggest news," Aramis answered with a small laugh.

"Were you surprised by this?" the man asked. "There

have been rumors for years that you and Elias may have children from your party days."

"We always dismissed them as rumors. My brother, by his own account, has always been very careful. I knew I hadn't been a couple of times, but never in my wildest dreams did I think I produced a son."

"How was it keeping this secret for so long, Esmée, and why did you?"

"It was definitely not easy," she said. "But I wanted to protect The Crown and my son from media attention. I didn't want him to be known as the Prince's bastard and figured it should be kept a secret."

"Why did you decide to tell him now?"

"I suffered a pretty bad accident recently and realized that I may not always be here to protect Oscar. I felt it was time for him to meet his father and for Aramis to know about him."

"How has it been for you, Oscar, to meet your father after all this time?"

"Good. Great. He's the best papa in the world." Oscar grinned. Everyone laughed.

"I have to ask, is there a chance the two of you will be together?" the interviewer asked. I held my breath, though I couldn't imagine why. It was a ridiculous, hopeless, fairy-tale question. Life wasn't a fairy tale though.

"I knew that question was coming." Aramis chuckled.

"No one knows what the future holds," Esmée said with a smile and a small shrug. I felt my entire body grow

hot. The burn of jealousy threatened to overtake me. I counted to ten in my head. It was a trick King Elias used often and I desperately needed it to work.

"It doesn't bother you that the Prince is featured in all of the tabloids with various women, most recently with his long-time friend and secretary?"

"Definitely not. He has a colorful past. I mean," Esmée signaled at Oscar and laughed. "But I don't believe either one of them ever confirmed that romance. People kiss all the time."

"So, there is hope for a reconciliation?" the interviewer asked. Aramis and my eyes met briefly, but he quickly looked away and back at the interviewer.

"It wouldn't be a reconciliation. We had a one-night stand eight years ago and created this wonderful child." Aramis smiled.

"So, it would be a new romance," the interviewer said. "The people have followed all of your romances closely through the years and are always curious to know what kind of woman it would take for you to settle down with."

"It would take a very strong woman to settle down with me, definitely. One who is willing to look past my flaws and accept me for who I am. I'm not as picky as people think I am. I don't need an heiress or a socialite. I want what everyone else wants, to be loved unconditionally." He shrugged a shoulder.

"On that note, I guess we can definitely say that Esmée is a potential contender," the interviewer said with a laugh.

Esmée blushed and smiled wide.

Aramis laughed along.

The cameras cut.

I stormed outside.

I bypassed my cottage and walked right up to the first car available. When I saw Pierre standing there, talking to another one of the security guards, I signaled at the car. He must have been listening to the interview because it was as if he knew what was happening, or maybe he sensed how upset I was.

"Just drive." I buckled my seatbelt. "Drive. Drive. Drive."

Pierre set the car in drive and did as he was told. "Just aimlessly?"

"Yes, that's fine, I don't care." My heart was still pounding. Adrenaline was still shooting through my veins. I felt absolutely and completely heartbroken.

"Maybe you should just speak to him," Pierre suggested as he parked on the side of the road. We were surrounded by woods and it was beginning to snow, so I stayed put for a moment.

"I can't. What would I say? I mean, you heard him." My shoulders dropped. "God, I'm so stupid. I warned Addie not to get involved with someone in this family and here I am. Involved."

"For what it's worth, he didn't say he'd get together with Esmée. In fact, I think he made it clear that he wouldn't."

"She didn't seem to get the memo."

Pierre nodded. "I know you're half-French, but you're mostly English, wouldn't you say?"

"Yes. I mean, I grew up there, so yes."

"And you've never met anyone from these nearby towns, have you?"

"Not really, no. I mean, in passing, but not really met."

"Let me tell you something about them, for centuries, millennia, even, they've existed solely to serve The Crown. From the time of the Sun King, they were all at the mercy of those who lived inside of the palace walls. They were provided with jobs, and if they were called upon, they provided the King with whatever he asked. A lot of the women were called upon."

Pierre shot me a look. "The kings often took advantage of their power. Up until even King Elias's father. He had women brought in from various surrounding towns and well, use your imagination."

"What does that have to do with Esmée?"

"Esmée follows that tradition. It is her duty to serve The Crown. It would be her joy to be in Aramis's life, in whatever capacity. It used to be that women like her would end up as mistresses, but now with the media attention and the access everyone has, she doesn't have to settle for that. If she can go on television and basically stake her claim and get the people to root for her, she may just become his wife."

I let that sink in. I hated it even more than any of my previous thoughts. He wasn't wrong. We used the media to create narratives we approved of, so what Esmée did today was get ahead of that.

"I hate her."

"I don't blame you." Pierre smiled. "The good news is, Aramis doesn't buy into all of that. He doesn't care what the media says, what his family says, what his role in all of this is. He only serves himself. That should be enough for you to know that if he truly cares for you, he'll be with you."

"Why didn't he say that then?"

"How could he tell the world something he hasn't even told you yet?"

"How do you know he hasn't told me yet?"

"If he had, you wouldn't be so insecure about your relationship and he would have told the world."

"You're pretty smart, Pierre."

"Thank you." He chuckled.

We both turned to see one of the royal SUVs pull up beside us. My eyes widened when I saw Aramis get out of the driver's seat. He looked like a bull ready for a fight. I lowered my window.

"Do you need something?"

"As a matter of fact, I do, but apparently you're busy."

"I'm busy? Aren't you supposed to be having lunch with your potential future wife and son?" I raised an eyebrow, feeling every single ounce of anger flood back.

"Maybe you should go back with him," Pierre suggested. "So you can talk."

Aramis's jaw ticked. I put the window back up.

"Thank you for humoring me." I looked at Pierre and opened the door, stepping out and waiting until he drove back in the direction of the palace. Aramis was still mad when I looked at him.

"What?"

"What?" he snapped. "You disappeared and then I find you in a car with Pierre and you think that's just fine?"

"Why wouldn't it be? Pierre is my friend."

"Yeah, he's my friend too but I don't feel the need to go off into the woods with him. If he was just a friend you could speak to him in public."

"I was trying to get away from you." My voice was getting higher with each word. Not even the snow that was starting to fall around us could cheer me up this time. "I didn't want to distract you in front of your potential girlfriend."

"What are you . . . Esmée?" He blinked. "Are you serious?"

"She wants to be with you. She wants you to be a big happy family and she ensured the public would be rooting for that by saying what she did in that live interview." I pointed toward the Palace.

"And what do you want, Joslyn?"

"It doesn't matter what I want!"

"It matters to me."

"I want what's best for The Crown."

"Fuck The Crown. I'm asking what you want." He stepped closer still, until he was looming over me, covering my face so the snowflakes were no longer falling on it.

"It doesn't matter what I want." I shook my head softly.

"Let me tell you what I want then, since no one has ever fucking asked me that question." He grabbed both my arms. "I want you. You, Joslyn. You're the only one I want in my life. Fuck what the media says. Fuck what Esmée says. Fuck what my mother or brother or sister-in-law say. I want you." He pressed his lips against me, closing the statement between us as if it needed to be caught there, where no one else would take it away. I reached up and wrapped my arms around his neck, deepening the kiss.

"I want you as well," I said against his lips. "I want you so much, it hurts."

"The feeling is mutual." He searched my eyes. "I'm serious. I don't want to live without you. I want you to be my girlfriend, my fiancée, my wife, whatever it takes to keep you."

"Really?"

"Really." He smiled slightly. "If you'll have me."

"Of course I'll have you." I smiled back.

"Will you come back to the main house with me? Have lunch with my son and his mother?"

"I don't like her." I groaned, throwing my head back. "I know it's childish, but I don't."

"You don't have to like her. I mean, I wish you would, of course, but as long as you both have a mutual respect and know that neither of you is going anywhere, I don't care if you like her."

"She'll want to become your mistress."

"What?" Aramis let out a surprised laugh.

"If she can't have you as a boyfriend or a husband, she'll want you in another capacity."

"Joslyn." He held my chin high to keep my attention. "If I wanted to have a mistress, I'd stay single and keep playing the field. I've already done that. I'm tired of it. Bored of it. Let me try to keep one woman happy."

"As long as I'm that woman."

"Forever and always." He kissed me again, softly. "Can we get out of the cold now?"

"Yes." I laughed and followed him to the car.

CHAPTER THIRTY

GROANED AT THE SIGHT OF THE HEADLINE ON THE FRONT PAGE of the paper: "Prince torn between two loves."

"This is all Esmée's fault," I said for the third time.

"She realizes that," Aramis said, finishing his bowtie. "She'll be here tonight."

"You invited her to the gala?"

"Of course. Why wouldn't I?"

"Because . . . I don't know I could think of a million reasons, which one do you want first?"

He chuckled, kissing the top of my head. "You look stunning, by the way."

"I didn't think you noticed." I glanced at him over my shoulder, showing off my exposed back.

"Notice? I'm trying not to look at you too much. Too many filthy thoughts are running rampant in my brain right now. I'm trying to figure out what room will be vacant so I can fuck you in it in the middle of the gala."

My stomach flipped. I bit my lip. "I think the library will be empty."

"I think I've already pictured you naked in every single corner of the library." His gaze darkened.

"You do realize that was where you took my virginity?" I raised an eyebrow.

"How could I forget?" He walked toward me, cupping the side of my face. "I want you to marry me, Joslyn."

"What?" I gasped. "You're not serious."

"I am so serious. I've been thinking about this a lot."

Despite the way my stomach somersaulted, I simply kissed him and met his eyes. "You'll have to ask me again, on one knee."

"On one knee?" He laughed. "That's a requirement?"

"I believe so."

He kissed me again. "Noted."

We finished getting dressed in silence. He hadn't even said he loved me. Not yet. Not that I'd said it to him either. It was just assumed and obviously if he wanted to marry me I could definitely assume that he did love me but I wanted to hear it. For some reason the thought of him saying those three words was a big deal. Maybe because I knew he'd never said them. Maybe because I knew I was the one who had actually managed to capture his heart and undying attention. The fact that he wanted to marry me should have been enough, but I wanted to hear the words.

"I see you're not caught between two loves," an older man said to Aramis as we stepped off the dance floor.

"I'm very much only caught in one." Aramis smiled, squeezing my hand. "You know the papers will say whatever it takes to sell more."

"Absolutely." He smiled at me. "I'm thrilled to see him settled down and happy for once. Congratulations."

"Thank you." I felt myself frown as I said the words and watched him walk away. "It's kind of strange for someone to congratulate me when you're the one who lucked out."

Aramis laughed loudly, throwing his head back. "I can't say I disagree."

"There you two are." That was Elias. "I want to introduce you to someone . . ."

I lost track of what he was saying because I caught a glimpse of Adeline clutching the chair beside her and holding her belly. I must have gasped, because both men turned to me.

"What's the matter?" Aramis asked.

"I think Adeline is going into labor."

We all rushed toward her and what followed was a blur. There were shouts and shuffling and soon enough we found ourselves in the back of the SUV headed to the hospital.

"Is she doing all right?"

"She's doing great." I glanced over at Esmée, who was sitting in the chair beside me with a boot instead of a cast, and smiled.

Adeline was doing perfectly fine and the baby was as well. Prince Louis. I smiled at the name. Smiled because my friend got all of her wishes—the unconditional love of a husband and an adorable, healthy baby. It was more than I'd ever thought about for myself, but I knew Addie wanted both of those things. I'd always been very pragmatic when it came to the idea of marriage. I knew it was something I wanted to do, but I wasn't actively thinking about it. The same went for kids. I wasn't even positive I wanted any of my own, but I figured when I met the right person I would re-evaluate.

"I owe you an apology," Esmée said.

"What for?" I turned to her once more, this time tentatively.

"The television interview. The way I treated you in my house." She offered a small smile. "I guess I stupidly thought there was a chance that Aramis would see me as more than just a one-night stand, or the mother of his child, you know?"

"I've never tried to sabotage a relationship, so, no, I don't know."

"I'm sorry." She glanced down at her hands. "I have no excuse. It won't happen again."

"In that case, apology accepted."

"Really?" She looked surprised when our eyes met again.

I shrugged a shoulder. "We can't be enemies and be on the same team when it comes to Oscar."

"I'm glad you're in his life." She smiled. "I'm glad you're in all of our lives."

"Thank you. That means a lot." I looked at her boot. "When does that come off?"

"Not for another two months." She sighed heavily. "My bones hate me."

"That's awful." I cringed. "At least you get to walk around a little better."

"That is definitely a plus."

"No more climbing on top of ladders though."

"Definitely not." She laughed. "I think my father would knock me off himself. I'm surprised he hasn't tied me to the couch so I don't move." She rolled her eyes.

"It's good that he looks after you." I smiled.

"I guess it is."

My own parents were free spirits. Such free spirits that

I wasn't sure they'd take care of me at all if something like that happened to me. They were busy traveling the world. Currently on a sailboat. I'd learned to accept that long ago and even though my friends used to think it was disturbing that they were like that, it definitely taught me that I didn't want to be that person in life in general. It wasn't only about parenting to me, it was about being present.

Aramis and Oscar walked down the hall back to where we were.

Oscar ran up to us. "The baby is so small. Tiny. The size of my head!"

"He can't be that small," Esmée said, laughing.

"He's a tiny little thing," Aramis said, smiling wide. He reached out for my hand. I took it and stood. "They're ready for you."

"I can't wait to meet him."

"I think we'll get going." Esmée stood as well. "I promised Papa we'd have supper with him after Oscar met his cousin."

"They're ready," Aramis said to the security guard standing closest to us before looking at Oscar again. "I'll see you this weekend, okay?"

"See you this weekend." Oscar wrapped his arms around Aramis's legs, then my waist. "We're going to have so much fun and we're going to have ice cream." He turned to his mother and gave her his hand.

"Ice cream? Wow." Esmée smiled and waved goodbye to us as she walked toward the security.

Aramis pulled me down the hall quietly and pushed open the door where Adeline, Elias, Adeline's mother and father, and The Queen Mother were. There was a bundle in Adeline's arms. I let go of Aramis and walked closer, unable to take my eyes off the baby.

"He is small," I whispered.

"You want to carry him?" Addie asked.

I shook my head. "I'll wait until he's home."

"Come on, Joss. How are you not going to carry my baby?"

"Trust me, I will, but he literally just exited your vagina. I think he needs a moment to acclimate to the world first." I leaned over him and tugged the blanket softly out of his little mouth, smiling at the tiny bubbles of spit there. "He is so, so, so, so cute."

"He's perfect." That was Aramis, who walked forward and wrapped an arm around me.

"And Addie. Addie was so perfect," Elias added, unable to keep the pride from his voice. "Such a natural. The doctor even said it."

"Did anyone call Pilar?" the Queen Mother asked, taking out her cell phone. "I'm going to video call."

Soon, Pilar and Ben appeared on her phone screen. They were in Fiji for their honeymoon and both looked like they'd been laying out in the sun the entire time they'd been there.

"The baby!" Pilar squealed. "Oh my God, I knew we were going to miss the birth. Let me see. Let me see."

The Queen Mother walked over to the bed with her phone and showed them. Pilar and Ben cooed and spoke to the baby and Adeline for a short while. I couldn't seem to stop staring at the little bundle. I felt a hand on my shoulder.

"Soon you'll have one of those." It was Mademoiselle Rose.

"I don't know." I smiled as I looked at her.

"You don't know?" Aramis asked. "Can't you picture little Joslyns and Aramises running around?"

"Can you?" I glanced up at him, surprised at the way he said it.

"Definitely." He kissed the top of my head.

"I hear wedding bells," Mademoiselle Rose said.

"Not yet." I felt myself blush.

"You're not getting any younger." That was Pilar, via video call.

"We're not in the eighteen-hundreds anymore." I rolled my eyes at her, but smiled because I knew she was joking and if I was being completely honest with myself, I was smitten with Aramis and so happy that he wanted all of these things with me.

When we got back to Versailles later that night, we sat in front of the cottage fireplace with wine in our hands, nibbling on some cheese.

"I can't believe my best friend had a baby today," I said. "And my other best friend is on her honeymoon."

"Yeah, imagine one of those being your little sister and the other being your older brother."

"I never thought of it like that." I laughed, looking over at him. "How does that make you feel?"

"Old?" He chuckled. "It used to make me feel inadequate, but I'm happy with the way things are going right now."

"Me too."

"I guess I needed them to move along with their lives for me to realize that the way I was living mine wasn't ideal."

"It definitely wasn't." I sighed, leaning back onto the couch. "Do you think when we get back to Paris you'll go back to your partying ways?"

"Why would I do that?"

"I don't know." I met his gaze. "Why did you do anything before?"

"Attention. Boredom. Inadequacy." He checked each reason off with his fingers. "I didn't have you."

"As I recall, I was picking up after your messes during each one of those parties."

"As I recall, all I wanted was for you to slap me and then kiss me and send me to my room."

"I definitely wanted to slap you." I laughed.

"I wasn't opposed."

"Really, though, do you think you'll go back to your old ways?" I wasn't sure why I was so stuck on this.

Maybe I needed reassurance that this wasn't a fling that was tied to this place and this holiday. I needed to know that we wouldn't go back to the same old thing, with us at odds with each other because I couldn't handle his stupid decisions and he couldn't handle me calling him out for them. Aramis set his glass down and took mine out of my hand and set it down beside his before turning toward me.

"Hey." He lifted my chin with his pointer. "I have zero interest in going back to partying. If I attend a party, it'll be with you by my side. If I host one, it'll be with you by my side. If I do anything from now on, I want it to be with you by my side."

"Okay," I whispered.

"What's brought this on?"

"I just . . ." I moved my face so that it wasn't a prisoner to his hand, but still looked at him again. "I'm serious about us, and I know you say you are as well, but I don't want this to be a holiday fling."

"Joss." He cocked his head. "I'm in love with you. So in love with you that I don't want to spend five minutes apart from you. This is not a holiday fling."

"Dammit, Aramis." I threw my arms around his neck and kissed him. He laughed against my lips.

"Was that what you needed to hear?"

"I guess so." I nodded, smiling.

"I love you." His expression grew serious again. "I love you and I want to be with you forever."

"I love you too."

I kissed him again and the wine was forgotten, the cheese was forgotten, and the fire in front of us was replaced by the one between us.

CHAPTER THIRTY-ONE

We'd been in Paris for two months and I'd spent the majority of my time overseeing the construction in Aramis's apartment. He decided that he wanted a new apartment, but instead of putting this one up for sale and buying another, he had a team gut the entire thing from the kitchen to the master bedroom. We'd been vacillating between my apartment and his whenever we had to be there too early to not sleep there for the better part of two months. I was looking at this week's schedule when he walked in with his mother trailing closely behind.

"There is entirely too much dust in this place, Aramis." She looked around and shook her head.

"Why do you think we've been staying at Joslyn's place?"

She looked at me. "Maybe you two should stay at my place. I'll be in Spain for a few weeks."

"We don't mind. It's a short drive to my apartment."

"Short drive? With no traffic maybe and when is there ever no traffic?"

She wasn't wrong.

"Besides, you'll be closer to Adeline and Elias."

"That's true."

"You can help with the baby while I'm away."

"I'm pretty sure they have nannies," Aramis said.

"Nannies they don't even take advantage of. You know Adeline wants to be hands-on. I don't think that woman has gotten sleep in months."

"She's not wrong," I said. "Maybe we should help out more often."

"Her mother is there," Aramis said.

"Her mother has been in London for a month now. She has too many events coming up."

"We were over there last night and they seemed fine," Aramis said.

"Addie looked tired. She's not going to complain. You know her."

"Joslyn is right. Besides, all of the events you have lined up this week are closer to my house."

"That's true," I said.

"Fine then. We'll stay over there." Aramis looked at his mother. "When are you leaving?"

"I'm on my way to the airport now. I wanted to speak with you." She looked at me. "We'll just be a moment."

I nodded and grabbed my phone before walking out into the hall. There, I continued looking at the schedule for the week. It was more of the same—more classroom appearances, some cocktail events, and a few ribbon-cutting ceremonies. With Elias home with Adeline and the baby, Aramis and Pilar were left to take on a bigger role. The issue was that Pilar was traveling with Ben for some football appearances and that meant Aramis had to take on all of it. Before long, the door opened and the Queen Mother stepped out.

She smiled at me. "I'll be seeing you, Joslyn."

"Have a safe trip." I smiled back.

"Keep me posted on things here."

"I will. Try to relax a little. Everything will be fine over here."

"For the first time in a long time, I can truly say that I have no doubt about that." She stepped forward, closing the distance between us and patting my cheek. "Thank you for being so good to us."

"You don't need to thank me for that. That's what family is for."

She smiled wider and walked away. I walked back inside and went to Aramis's bedroom while he spoke to the construction people. Most of his things were already in my apartment, but I needed to make sure to grab some of his suits. After all, he couldn't wear the same ones he wore last week.

"Packing for me again?" he asked, walking into the closet.

"If I don't, who will?"

"I used to pack my clothes."

"When?" I blinked over at him. "Was this around the same time when you used to do your own laundry?"

"Funny." He chuckled. "You know I've never done my own laundry."

"So spoiled." I shook my head.

"Hey, I told you that you didn't have to do yours either. You're the control freak."

"Because I don't mind washing my own intimates?"

"I wouldn't mind washing your intimates." His gaze darkened, despite the playful smile on his face.

"Let's keep it PG. There's a crew of men in this house right now."

"Fine." He walked over and kissed me sweetly. "I'm ordering Indian food for us to have at my mother's house tonight."

"Perfect."

"In the meantime, do you want to help me pick out cabinets?"

"I feel like I've picked everything and this isn't even my house, but okay." I walked out of the closet and he followed.

He grinned. "We also need to pick the color of the grout."

"Are you just making me do this because you're regretting tearing this place apart?"

"Yes and no."

"Yes and no?" I laughed.

"Once it's finished, it'll be your place too."

"I have my own place." I raised an eyebrow at him.

"Are you completely opposed to breaking your lease?"

"Are you asking me to move in with you?"

"Yes." No hesitation.

"Then, the answer is yes."

"The food is here," I called out.

Aramis was taking an eternity in the shower. That's what it felt like anyway. We'd spent the rest of our day packing and then upstairs at Elias and Adeline's place. This family owned four buildings and all four buildings had the higher floors closed off for them alone. The rest of the floors were open for the rest of the family to buy, but even then there was a long checklist their uncles, aunts, and cousins needed to get through before they were allowed to move in. I was always curious as to how many people they'd said no to, but I didn't exactly want to ask any of them. I opened the door and took the food back to the table. My stomach was growling by the time I finished plating everything.

"Aramis?" I called out. "The food is going to get cold."

"I'll be right out."

I sighed, opening the bottle of wine he'd picked out for tonight. It looked fancy, expensive, but then, most things he picked out were. It was something I was used to, but still somehow surprised me each day. It was hard to explain. My parents had always been into the finer things, but they made a big deal out of them. Aramis kind of brushed off his riches because it was all he knew. I fixed the wine glasses on each of our place settings and stepped back to admire it all. When he finally showed up, I'd expected him to be wearing his favorite sweatpants and T-shirt. Instead, he was wearing jeans and a crisp dress shirt. I frowned.

"Are you going somewhere?"

"No. Why?"

"Why are you so . . . dressed?"

"Dressed?" He chuckled, sitting down at the head of the table. I was sitting to his right. "Would you rather me be naked?"

"I mean, I wouldn't be opposed." I shrugged. "But I mean, you're dressed, dressed."

"I'm starving." He started drinking some wine and serving his food, ignoring my question, but I was too busy staring at him to care about my food, despite my growling stomach. "You seem hungry."

"I am."

"So, eat."

"I'm trying to figure you out." I narrowed my eyes. "Are you going back to Elias's place to have a drink?"

"Maybe. Should I?"

"I don't know. I'm just trying to understand why you're dressed so nice."

"I'm wearing jeans."

"You know what I mean."

He sighed. "Fine."

"Fine what?"

"I was going to do this after dinner, but since you're so nosey and keep asking questions I guess I'll get on with it." He stood from his chair and got down on one knee beside me. I gasped, then gasped again, my heart hammering.

"Oh my God."

"Joslyn. You're the best thing in my life. I don't ever want to imagine being without you. Will you marry me?" He pulled out a ring, a massive diamond on a beautiful gold setting. "This is the ring my father gave my mother. It's the ring his father before his gave his wife, and his father before his gave his. It's been in my family for generations and I can't think of a more deserving, special person to give it to."

My mouth dropped as he started sliding it on my finger. I felt tears begin to trickle over my cheeks, but I couldn't understand why. I was so happy I felt like I was about to burst.

"Joss?"

"Yeah?" I wiped my cheeks.

"Will you marry me?"

"Yes," I shouted. "Oh my God. Yes!"

He finished setting the ring on my finger and laughed

as he kissed me. "I thought for a second you were going to say no."

"I'm just so . . . was that why your mother wanted to speak to you today? How many people know about this?"

"Basically everyone."

"Everyone?" I blinked. "Even Adeline?"

"Even Adeline."

"What!"

"They're pretty good at keeping secrets when they have to." He smiled.

"I can't believe we're getting married!" I looked at the ring again. "Are you sure I should have this ring? It feels . . . important."

"You're the most important person in my life. I'm absolutely sure you should have it."

"I just . . . wow."

"Fit for a beautiful princess."

I met his gaze again and the reality of all of this crashed down on me. "A princess."

"My princess." He smiled as he leaned in and kissed me softly.

ClaireContrerasbooks.com

Twitter: @ClariCon

Insta: ClaireContreras

Facebook: www.facebook.com/groups/
ClaireContrerasBooks

OTHER BOOKS

The Trouble With Love

Fake Love

The Consequence of Falling

Because You're Mine

Half Truths

The Sinful King

Twisted Circles

Fables & Other Lies

SECOND CHANCE DUET

Then There Was You

My Way Back to You

The Wilde One

The Player